The Case
of the Vanishing
Corpse

The Case
of the Vanishing
Corpse

by Robert Newman

AN ALADDIN BOOK
Atheneum

Published by Atheneum
All rights reserved
Copyright © 1980 by Robert Newman
Published simultaneously in Canada by McClelland & Stewart, Ltd.
Manufactured by Fairfield Graphics
Fairfield, Pennsylvania
ISBN: 0-689-71037-2
First Aladdin Edition

FOR JAY WILLIAMS
*who knew London so well
and loved it so much.*

Contents

PROLOGUE   ix

1. The Surprising Constable   3
2. Verna   20
3. The Denham Diamonds   29
4. Inspector Finch   50
5. The Second Robbery   70
6. The Baron and the Wild West Show   91
7. The Vanishing Corpse   106
8. Finch's Fury   119
9. The Watchers   141
10. The Chase   169
11. The Corpse Reappears   195
12. The Loose Ends   210

Prologue

Shaking the sistrum, the young woman danced gravely, sedately, her bare arms and legs gleaming in the light of the torches—and suddenly the marchioness was convinced that this night was going to be different from the others; that this time something was going to happen.

She wasn't sure why she felt that way. The ceremony had only been going on for a short while. Brother Ibrahim had finished his invocation and was sitting cross-legged on the dais with his eyes closed, concentrating. There was silence except for the tinkling of the sistrum, the pad of the dancing girl's bare feet. All this was familiar—and yet there was something different; a growing tension of which all of them there in the grotto seemed to be aware.

The marchioness glanced at Mrs. Van Gelder, who sat next to her. Usually poised and imperturbable, she was leaning forward, frowning, and the marchioness was certain that she too expected a manifestation.

Would it be Isis? The marchioness hoped so. She had

always been drawn to her. Perhaps it would be Isis in her role as the mother, holding the infant Horus as she did in the tomb painting they had seen in Karnak. If not Isis, then. . . .

Wait. Something was taking shape in the rear of the grotto; the darkness was becoming denser, more solid. Then suddenly, with a roar, a nightmare figure leaped out into the light of the torches. It was huge, unmistakably male and unmistakably evil. She caught a glimpse of a bestial face, of gleaming white fangs and hands like talons. Eyes wide with terror, the young dancer shrank back, screamed as the monstrous figure seized her—and then the torches went out.

The marchioness sat there rigid, frozen. No, she said to herself. It didn't happen. It couldn't happen.

It was only later, when the torches were relit and they discovered that the dancer was gone and they were all splashed with blood, that she realized it *had* happened.

The Case
of the Vanishing
Corpse

1

The Surprising Constable

Andrew's train arrived at Paddington at a little after two. The first person he saw when he looked out of the compartment window was Sara, better known as Screamer. She was halfway down the platform, near the barrier. He waved to her, she waved back, then people came between them and he lost sight of her. He was travelling with two other boys from school and it took a few minutes before they all got porters. As they started along the platform towards the luggage van, he looked for Sara again, but she was gone.

"Will you be wanting a cab?" the porter asked Andrew as he put his trunk on a barrow.

"I'm not sure," said Andrew. He glanced toward the barrier, and there was Fred, looking taller than he actually was in his uniform. "No, I'm being met."

Fred came up as Andrew surrendered his ticket.

"Good afternoon, Master Andrew," he said, touching the cockade on his shiny top hat.

"Good afternoon, Fred." He turned to the boys who had travelled down with him. "Can I take you anywhere?"

"You're for St. John's Wood, aren't you?" said Bragaw, the older of the two.

"Yes."

"We're going the other way, Belgravia and Kensington. Thanks, but we'll take a growler."

"Right. See you in September."

Andrew watched them go off, then said to Fred, "Didn't I see Sara out on the platform?"

"Probably. She was out there."

"Well, where did she go?"

"I don't know. She must be around someplace."

Fred had been a jockey—and a good one—before he became a coachman. This gave him a fairly high opinion of himself. As a result, though he was respectful to Andrew's mother, whom he admired enormously, he was very offhand with everyone else.

"This way, mate," he said to the porter.

As they moved off towards the exit, Sara reappeared from behind a column.

"There you are," said Andrew. "What was the idea of disappearing that way?"

"You were with someone."

"Two boys from school. What of it?"

4

She shrugged.

"That's no answer. Did you feel shy about meeting them?"

"I'm not shy about meeting anyone!" she said hotly. "I thought *you* might feel funny about introducing me."

"Why?"

"Because you told me how almost everyone at that precious school of yours felt about having anything to do with girls—even sisters. And sometimes even mothers."

"That's true. I did say something about that. But I'm not almost everyone. I'm me."

"And so of course you wouldn't have minded." Her statement was intended to be crushingly ironic, but there was a note of uncertainty in it.

"No, I wouldn't."

When the train had pulled in under the iron and glass roof of the station, Andrew had found himself comparing that arrival with the one a little less than a year before when he had come to London for the first time. He had known no one then, and London had been a frightening place. Now it was home.

But great as that change had been, the one that had taken place in Sara had been just as great and even more dramatic. When he had first met her, she had been a waiflike street urchin who spoke such broad Cockney that he could barely understand her. Now her speech was even more careful than his—that was Andrew's mother's doing—and in her straw hat and white muslin dress she looked as if she'd stepped out of a Gainsborough painting. Much as he liked the way she looked, however, he hoped she wasn't too changed in other ways. For there were too many things about the old Sara—or rather Screamer—that he had admired.

Flushing a little under his scrutiny, she said, "Got your eye full?"

He grinned. Those were the first words she had said to him when he had stared at her in front of Sherlock Holmes's lodgings on Baker Street—and she said them now as she had said them then—aggressively and nasally.

"No," he said. "But I think I may have by the time I go back to school." They went towards the exit. "How's your mother?"

"Fine."

"And Sam?"

"Fine too. He says studying is hard work, but I think he likes it."

"That's good."

Sam was Sara's brother—a little older than Andrew—who was now in Stubbington House in Fareham, studying for the examination that might allow him to become a naval cadet. That was Andrew's mother's doing too— that, and many other things, like the way she had made Sara's and Sam's mother the housekeeper at their new house—all to show her appreciation for what the Wigginses had done for Andrew when he had first arrived in London.

They were outside now, and there, between a hansom cab and a four-wheeler, was the Tillett's new landau. Fred had just put Andrew's bag and trunk into it, and the porter was leaving.

"Just a second," said Andrew, reaching into his pocket for a tip.

"Keep your hair on," said Fred. "I took care of him."

"Why should you?" asked Andrew.

"You don't think it was me own brass, do you?" said Fred. "Your mother gave it to me." He turned to the porter. "Are you all right, mate?"

"Right as ever went endwise," said the porter. He touched his cap to Sara and Andrew and went off whistling.

"In you get," said Fred, opening the polished black door for them. He closed the door, climbed up into the box, shook the reins and they moved off into the traffic that was going up Praed Street.

This was another of the things that was so new Andrew found it hard to believe; riding in his mother's carriage behind a pair of matched bays. And to make it perfect, the weather was warm and the landau's top was down. Andrew glanced at Sara and could tell that she was enjoying it as much as he was.

"Is my mother at the theatre?" he asked.

"Yes. They're having the dress rehearsal—that's why she couldn't come to the station. But she wants you to pick her up at about six."

Andrew nodded. "She wasn't too sure about the play before. How does she feel about it now."

"She thinks it's all right. That it might go."

"Might go?" said Fred from the box. "It's going to be a smasher!"

Smiling, Andrew exchanged glances with Sara.

"How do you know?" he asked.

"How do I know a Derby winner?" said Fred emphatically. "I seen some of the rehearsals. *And* I talked to some of the stage hands and the chap at the stage door. They think she's a ruddy marvel."

Like the carriage and the house in St. John's Wood, this was new to Andrew too. Until recently his mother had been away, playing on the continent and in America and he had known very little about her; certainly not that she was a well-known and successful actress. Though they had become very close since her return to England, he had never seen her on the stage. But he had seen the effect she had on people—men in particular— and was not surprised at Fred's enthusiastic admiration for her.

Her relationship with Sara was something else again. Verna herself had been born in Lambeth, the daughter of street musicians, and had come to the stage by way of the music halls. She undoubtedly saw herself in Sara, who was a brave, quick-witted child with natural acting ability; and so Verna had paid special attention to her—

her speech and dress and manners—when she took the Wiggins family under her wing.

"Have you anything else to tell me?" Andrew asked Sara.

"No."

"How's school?"

"Oh, all right. How's yours?"

"All right too."

"Your mother said you were playing a lot of cricket."

"Just on the house team."

They were just passing Lord's and Sara nodded to it and said, "Well, you won't have to travel very far if you want to watch any while you're at home."

"No. As a matter of fact, I want to see the Eton-Harrow match. Would you like to go?"

"Oh, yes!"

"I'll see what we can do about it."

They crossed Wellington Road and St. John's Wood High Street, turned left and a few minutes later they were at the house on Rysdale Road.

It was quite large, larger than most of the villas that lined the street; a three-story stucco house set well back from the road with a garden in front of it. Fred turned into the graveled driveway and stopped under the porte-cochere. Matson opened the door. He was quite tall and grey-haired, and he stooped slightly. Andrew had not understood why they needed a butler when they had

Mrs. Wiggins to supervise the running of the house, but Verna said it was expected of someone in her position. That may have been why Matson always looked slightly pained; because he was aware that his post was more ceremonial than anything else.

They went through the accepted ritual with Matson hoping that he had had a pleasant journey ("Yes, Matson. Thank you."), then went inside where Mrs. Wiggins and Annie, the upstairs maid, were waiting.

"Hello, Mrs. Wiggins," said Andrew.

"Welcome home, Andrew," said Mrs. Wiggins. Then abandoning dignity—and the ritual—in favor of honest emotion, she embraced him. "I'm that glad to see you!"

"And I to see you."

"Annie," said Matson, carefully avoiding looking at them, "will you help Fred take Master Andrew's things upstairs?"

"Yes, Mr. Matson," said Annie.

"I'll go up too," said Mrs. Wiggins. She went up the stairs with him, opened the door to his room. It was large and sunny, just across the hall from his mother's suite.

"I think you've got everything you'll want," said Mrs. Wiggins.

"I'm sure I have," said Andrew.

They waited while Fred and Annie brought in the trunk and bag, put them down and left.

"Would you like me to unpack for you?" asked Mrs. Wiggins.

"No, thank you. How are you?"

"I'm fine, just fine. You heard about Sam?"

"Sara told me he's working hard but doing well."

"Yes, he is. Everything's too good to be true, thanks to your mother. She's a wonderful woman."

"Yes, she is. But then so are you."

"Nonsense!"

"Well, mother and I think you are." He had gone over to the window and was looking out. "What's happening next door at the marchioness's?"

"Have they started already?" Mrs. Wiggins looked out also. "I guess they have."

Three Oaks, home of the Marchioness of Medford, was probably the largest estate in St. John's Wood. Surrounded by a high stone wall, it was several acres in area. Besides the imposing house, it had formal and informal gardens, lawns, greenhouses and a small lake. Usually quiet, for the marchioness was a bit of a recluse, there was a good deal of activity there now; gardeners were working on the already carefully tended grounds and other men were setting up two large marquees.

"She's opening up the house and grounds tomorrow," said Mrs. Wiggins. "For charity, some hospital or foundling home or something. I think your mother's expecting to go. Would you like some tea?"

"I don't think so, thank you. I understand I'm to meet my mother at the theatre at six."

"That's right."

"I think I'll take a walk, look around, till it's time to leave." He opened the door. "Do you know where Sara is?"

"Probably in her room."

"Oh, Sara!" he called. Sara's room was at the end of the hall, near the back of the house. After a moment the door opened.

"Yes?" she said, looking at him oddly.

"I'm going for a walk. Want to come with me?"

She glanced at her mother, then looked at him again.

"Are you sure you want me?" she asked.

"Would I ask you if I didn't? Come on."

Again she glanced at her mother, then she came toward him, and they went down stairs together.

"What was that all about?" he asked when they were outside.

"What was what?"

"Whatever was going on between you and your mother."

"I don't know what you're talking about."

"Stop it, Screamer. Of course you know. Now what is it?"

He had called her Screamer deliberately—to remind her of the things they had done together less than a year ago. And apparently it had an effect.

"She said, if she let me go meet you at Paddington, then that was that. I wasn't to follow you around or expect you to spend any time with me."

"Why not?"

"I don't know."

"Screamer!"

"All right. Because I'm a girl, and boys don't like to be with girls, not until they're much older, and besides I'm younger than you. But most important of all—" She broke off.

"Yes?"

"Nothing."

"Screamer, the most important thing of all can't be nothing. Now what is it?" Her face stony, she did not look at him.

"All right. If you won't tell me, I'll tell you. It's because your mother's our housekeeper, so it's not proper."

"That's right."

"You mean I guessed what she said to you, but it's certainly not right. It's all wrong. Some boys may not like to be with girls, but I'm not some boys. I told you that at the station. And I don't care that you're a little younger than I am. As for this housekeeper thing, did it matter who I was and who you were when I first came to London and you took me in, took care of me?"

"Because we didn't know who you were—you didn't know yourself—though I knew you were a toff."

"Well, I knew who you were—you were my friends.

And my mother knew it too, and that's why she asked you to come here. So let's not have any more of this nonsense."

"It's not nonsense!" said Sara forcefully. "I don't want you to do me any favors!"

"Well, I'd like you to do me a favor. I'd like you to stop talking rot! If I ask you to come out for a walk with me, it's because I want you to!"

"Well, all right then," said Sara more quietly. They looked sideways at one another and when Andrew smiled at her, Sara flushed and finally smiled also.

They were out on Rysdale Road now, approaching the high stone wall that surrounded Three Oaks.

"I hear there's going to be a big do in there tomorrow," said Andrew.

"A quid to get in," said Sara. "But that includes tea or bubbly."

"How do you know?"

"I heard the marchioness's head groom telling Fred. Your mother's going."

"Why? She doesn't know the marchioness, does she?"

"No. But since it's for charity she thinks it's the neighborly thing to do."

Andrew was thinking about this, wondering why she should want to be neighborly, when a barrel organ began playing somewhere behind them. They turned, the music got louder, and a street musician came around the corner and into Rysdale Road. He was a slight, dark man with a large mustache. He was wearing a brown velvet jacket, baggy trousers and a black felt hat with a feather in it, and sitting on his shoulder, dressed exactly as he was, was a small monkey.

"Coo! Lumme! A hurdy-gurdy man!" said Sara, months of practice in proper speech forgotten in her excitement. "Have you got ha'penny for him?"

"I think so," said Andrew.

They walked back toward him. As they approached, the monkey leaped to the top of the barrel organ, from there to the ground and held up a tin cup. Andrew took some coins out of his pocket but when Sara said, "Oh, let me!" he gave them to her and she dropped them into the monkey's cup.

"*Grazie, signorina,*" said the organ grinder, bowing. "*Grazie, signor.*"

He pulled on the cord that was fastened to the monkey's belt, and the monkey bowed too, taking off it's hat, then leaped back to the organ and from there to the man's shoulder again.

"Will you play something for us?" asked Sara.

"*Con piacere,*" said the musician. He began turning the crank of the organ and the strains of "Funiculi, funicula" echoed along the quiet street. Her face rapt, Sara closed her eyes and began dancing as she must have danced dozens of times before when she was a dirty-faced street urchin living in Dingell's Court. Andrew watched her, admiring—not just her grace—but the way she forgot where she was and how she was dressed, everything but the music and what she was doing. He had a feeling that when his mother was Sara's age she had danced in the streets of Lambeth just as Sara was doing now.

But this wasn't Dingell's Court or Lambeth. It was Rysdale Road in St. John's Wood.

Heavy footsteps sounded on the pavement.

"Now then," said an official voice. "That'll be all of that. Pack it up and move along there."

The music stopped in the middle of a phrase, Sara opened her eyes, and she and Andrew looked up at the policeman.

"*Si signor*," said the organ grinder. "*Si, si*."

"Oh, no!" said Sara.

"Why does he have to move along?" asked Andrew. "He's not bothering anyone."

"I assume you can read," said the policeman, pointing to the notice on the wall of Three Oaks that said, "Hawkers, Circulars, Barrel-Organs and Street Cries of any Description Strictly Prohibited."

"Yes, I can read," said Andrew. "But I think it's jolly unfair to tell people what they can do and what they can't do out in the street!"

"For a slow bowler," said the policeman, "you're certainly quick to challenge the status quo."

"What?" said Andrew. "How do you know I'm a slow bowler?"

"How do I know that you're just home from school and that the young lady has lived elsewhere most of her life, probably near Edgeware Road? Elementary, my dear friends." And he started to walk on.

"Wait a minute!" said Andrew, hurrying after him. "That's what *he* used to say!"

"He?"

"Sherlock Holmes," said Andrew. He stopped in front of the policeman and looked up at him. "Who are you?"

"Constable Wyatt."

"Are you sure?" asked Andrew. Among other things, Holmes had been famous for his disguises. But there was no chance that this was Holmes. The policeman's eyes were blue, not grey. He was fair, not dark. And though he was as tall as Holmes, he was heavier and several years younger.

"Quite sure," said the policeman. "I'm sorry." When he smiled he looked younger than ever and less like a policeman.

"Are you really a policeman?" asked Sara.

"Really. Presently attached to B division, Wellington Road Police Station."

"Well, you don't look like a copper and you don't talk like one," said Sara flatly.

"That, my dear, is one of my crosses," said Constable Wyatt. He looked over his shoulder. "Our musician seems to have scarpered."

They looked too and saw the little Italian and his monkey disappearing around the corner.

"I don't care about that anymore," said Andrew. "But I do care about this. There's something strange about it." He frowned at Wyatt, then it came to him. "You know Holmes!"

Wyatt's smile became even broader. "Deduced like a true Holmesian disciple. Yes, I do know him, had the pleasure of talking to him on quite a few occasions."

"And he told you about us?" said Sara.

"He pointed you out from his window one day, said the two of you had been very helpful to him on one of his cases. The rest I deduced myself or got from talking to your coachman, Fred."

"What were you talking to Fred about?" asked Andrew.

"A case I'm on."

"Then you're a detective too," said Sara.

"Unfortunately, no. I'm just doing some legwork for Inspector Finch."

"What's the case?" asked Andrew.

"The disappearance of a young woman named Lily Snyder some four days ago."

"Around here?"

"Yes. We found a cabby who took her to Wellington Place at about six in the afternoon on Monday. You weren't here so you couldn't have seen her," he said to Andrew. "But did you, by any chance?" he asked Sara. "An attractive girl in her early twenties, brown hair, wearing a white shirtwaist, navy blue jacket and skirt and a black hat?"

"No," said Sara. "She's been gone since Monday?"

"Yes. And I'm afraid—"

"Wyatt!" said a sharp, authoritative voice. They turned. A short, aggressive-looking man in a bowler stood under one of the streetlights on the other side of Rysdale Road. He beckoned peremptorily.

"Finch," said Wyatt under his breath. "I've got to go, but I'll see you again." And he crossed the street, saluting as he approached the inspector.

"I wanted to ask him about Mr. Holmes," said Andrew. "I'd like to see him while I'm in London."

"He said we'd see him again," said Sara. "Constable Wyatt, I mean. I liked him."

"So did I."

2

Verna

Andrew changed his clothes, and a little after five he walked around to the stable, which was behind the house. Fred was just bringing the landau out.

"Why'd you come back here?" he asked.

"I didn't know what time we were going to leave."

"I would have come round when it was time. Why don't you try acting like a gentleman instead of a school-boy?"

"Why don't you try acting like a coachman instead of the Earl Marshall?"

Fred threw a punch at him, Andrew blocked it, and they sparred for a minute, then quit, grinning at one another. However Fred would not let Andrew sit in the box with him and handle the ribbons as he did sometimes when they were alone, insisting that it was not proper when they were going to call for his mother. So Andrew sat in back and they talked as Fred drove over to Regent's Park, around it and down Baker Street. The curtains were drawn on the windows of Sherlock Holmes's rooms but that didn't mean anything; Holmes often kept them drawn when he was talking to a client or thinking about a particularly puzzling case.

Fred told him that they had a new horse—a three-year-old hunter that Fred had picked out himself—which Andrew's mother rode several mornings a week. Andrew could ride it when she didn't and, if they wanted to ride together, Fred had arranged to borrow a gelding from the marchioness's groom who, like almost everyone in the area, seemed to be a pal of Fred's.

They arrived at the theatre, which was on the Strand, at a few minutes before six. The marquee already said: Verna Tillett in THE SQUIRE'S DAUGHTER. This gave Andrew a queer feeling but did not affect him as much as the posters on either side of the theatre entrance that carried large pictures of his mother. Fred took him around to the stage door and introduced him to the watchman, who touched his cap and conducted him along the dusty corridor that smelled of paint to his mother's dressing room. He knocked and when she responded, he opened the door and went in.

She was sitting at her dressing table with her back to him, but she was looking up, waiting, and their eyes met in the mirror. Before this she had always been rather tentative, studying him to determine whether he would object before she kissed him. But their separation since the Christmas holidays had been the longest they'd had since they had found one another and this time she did not wait. She rose, turned and embraced him.

"It's good to see you again," she said.

"It's good to see you."

She held him at arm's length. "How are you?"

"Fine. And you?"

"Fine too. You've grown since I last saw you. You're as tall as I am now."

"I think I am."

There was a discreet cough and they both looked at the man who stood in the corner of the room. He was grey-haired, but his face was young and he was slim and very elegant in his cape and evening clothes.

"I'm sorry," said Verna. "Darling, I don't think you know Mr. Harrison, the theatre manager. My son, Andrew."

"It's nice to meet you, Andrew."

"It's nice to meet you, sir."

"I've heard a great deal about you, and I'm delighted that you'll be here for your mother's opening."

"He's not coming to the opening!" said Verna.

"He's not?"

"Certainly not. He's never seen me on stage and I'm going to be nervous enough tomorrow night without having him here. He and Sara can come some night next week if the play's still running then."

"It'll be running, not just next week and next month, but next year. Your mother's absolutely splendid," he said to Andrew. "I'm very proud to be presenting her."

"You can see why Lawrence is so successful," said Verna to Andrew. Then to Harrison, "You're sure about tonight?"

"Positive. The few places I wasn't entirely happy about involved Fanny and Rupert, but not you. I'm going in to talk to them now. You have your supper with Andrew, then go home and I'll see you tomorrow night."

"One usually works until very late before an opening," she explained to Andrew. "And I was determined to see you even if we had to have supper sent in. But the dress went well enough so that we can go out."

"It went so well that I'm worried," said Harrison. "You know that a bad dress means a good performance and vice versa."

"Don't be so superstitious," said Verna.

"Can't help it. Where are you eating, by the way?"

"I think Rule's."

"Oh. I have an appointment at the Savoy. But then you probably want to be alone with Andrew."

"I certainly do."

"Until tomorrow then."

He said good night to them both and left. Verna glanced in the mirror, wiped a last trace of powder from her face and said, "Did you have tea?"

"No."

"You must be starved. We'll go right out."

Andrew helped her on with her cloak and they went out, saying good night to the watchman who opened the door for them. Fred saluted Verna as if she were royalty, drove them the short distance to the restaurant.

Though Andrew had never been to Rule's before, he knew it was the oldest theatrical restaurant in London, and it was obvious that Verna was known there, for the head waiter greeted her as deferentially as Fred had and showed them to a booth under a portrait of Mrs. Siddons as Lady Macbeth. They ordered prawns and grilled mutton chops with fresh strawberries to follow, then Verna said, "Now tell me everything that's happened since I saw you last."

"Nothing very much happened. I'd rather hear about you."

"There's plenty of time for that. Why do you say nothing happened? You had a good cricket season, didn't you?"

"Fairly good. We won five out of six matches."

Andrew had meant what he said: he did not feel that anything particularly interesting had happened during the time that he had been away and he had not intended to talk about either cricket or school. But Verna's questions were so pertinent and her responses so genuine that before he knew it he was telling her about both and a great many other things beside. They had just finished their chops and Verna was smiling at his account of a

Latin class for which no one was prepared, when a strik-
ing-looking man entered the restaurant. He was tall and
thin, with reddish hair and a short red beard, and he was
wearing a tweed Norfolk jacket. He started toward the
rear of the restaurant, saw Verna and paused at their
table.

"Miss Tillett," he said with a slight Irish accent.

"Good evening, Mr. Shaw."

"And who is my rival?" he asked, fixing Andrew with
a bright blue eye.

"My son, Andrew."

"Oh? Good evening, Andrew."

"Good evening, sir."

"I didn't realize that you were married," he said to
Verna.

"I'm not."

"Sorry. If you insist on being a purist, I didn't realize
that you *had* been married."

"I wasn't being a purist. I was stating a fact—which is
that I am neither a widow nor a divorcée."

The bearded man looked at her with quiet admiration,
then turned to Andrew.

"Are you aware, Andrew," he said, "that your mother
is one of the most interesting women in London?"

"Yes, sir."

"Good for you. It's the kind of perception I would
expect from her son. As for you, Miss Tillett, may I in-
form you that though the theatre is not my usual sphere

of activity, I have asked to be allowed to review your play tomorrow night."

"I'm flattered, though I'm afraid your talent will be wasted. Mr. Howard, the playwright, is not exactly Ibsen."

"My talents will not be wasted because I expect yours to be conspicuous. As for the play, I doubt that you will find one worthy of you till I write it myself."

"And will that be soon?"

"Now that I have found my heroine, a true 'new woman,' it may be. Good night—and good luck tomorrow night." Bowing, he went on.

"Do you have a good memory, Andrew?" asked Verna.

"Fairly good."

"Then remember this moment. For you have just met the cleverest man in London, probably in England."

"Mr. Shaw?"

"George Bernard Shaw."

"And he writes about the theatre?"

"He hasn't so far. He has written brilliant art and music criticism for the *Star* and the *World*, but we've talked about the theatre several times and I'm fascinated by the thought that he's going to review my play. Because I'm convinced that it's in the theatre that he's going to make his name."

Andrew nodded. He had liked Mr. Shaw, who had treated him like an adult. But what he had liked most about him was his obvious and sincere admiration of Verna; admiration that Andrew shared. For how many women were there who, without explanation or embarrassment, would insist on making it clear that they were not and never had been married?

Not that Andrew had always been so understanding. When he had first heard the story of his father's death, it had created serious problems for him and he had had even more serious difficulties in accepting the fact of his illegitimacy. But, in the end, he had accepted it, and that was one of the reasons he and his mother were now so close. However, that was also the reason he had no close friends at school. He not only felt he was different from most boys his age, he found that many of his ideas were different from theirs. For instance, he did not mind espousing unpopular causes and on most issues he sided with the underdog. If he had been less secure, less bright in his studies and less of a cricket player, all this would have made him seem like a very odd fish indeed. But, as it was, it made him all the more interesting to the other boys and to the masters.

By the time they had finished their strawberries, the excitement and fatigue of the long day had begun to catch up with Andrew. Verna noticed it, called for the bill, and they left. Fred, waiting outside in Maiden Lane, drove them home, and Matson let them in. By that time Andrew had recovered somewhat and insisted that he would like to stay up and talk, but now Verna claimed that she was tired—she had a long and difficult day ahead of her—and so they said good night. Andrew fell asleep almost immediately. He woke once during the night, wondering what time it was, heard the grandfather clock out on the landing strike two and prepared to go to sleep again when he heard something else: a faint but clear whistle somewhere outside, probably near where the wall of Three Oaks abutted on their garden. He had a feeling that perhaps he should get up, see who was whistling and why, but before he could do so he fell asleep again.

3

The Denham Diamonds

Andrew had breakfast alone the next morning, helping himself to bacon and eggs from the silver dishes on the buffet and eating at the round table that overlooked the garden. He was feeling very adult and worldly, for the morning paper, neatly folded, had been put next to his place, and though he never looked at it at other times, he was reading it when Sara came in.

"Good morning," he said. "Had breakfast?"

"Hours ago with mum." She didn't come any closer, stood just inside the doorway, looking at him oddly.

"Anything wrong?"

"No. It's just that I've only seen grown-ups read the paper before this. My father used to when he was still alive. And Matson and Fred do here."

"If Fred reads anything, it's the racing results. But I'm sure my mother reads it, too."

"I guess she does. Mum puts *The Times* on the tray when Annie takes it up to her. But since she always has breakfast in her room" . . . She edged closer to the table. "Is there anything in it?"

"Lot's of things. But," he nodded toward the article he had been reading, "this is particularly interesting."

"What is it?"

"A story about that missing girl Constable Wyatt told us about yesterday."

"Read it to me."

"Come on, Sara. You can read it yourself. Mother tells me you're doing very well in school."

"All right. Let's see."

She took the paper and looked at the story he had indicated. It was captioned *Missing Girl Traced to St. John's Wood*.

"A spokesman for the Metropolitan Police has announced that Lily Snyder, missing since Monday, has been traced to St. John's Wood. A cabman has been found who remembers taking her to Wellington Road and St. John's Wood High Street at about six o'clock in the evening. It is possible that she made other visits to the vicinity for another cab driver has informed the police that he took a woman answering to her description to the same area about a week before. Miss Snyder, twenty-one years old, brown-haired and attractive, worked as a waitress at the Cafe de Paris in Leicester Square and also occasionally posed for artists as a model. Though most of London's best known painters and sculptors live in Chelsea, a few live in St. John's Wood.

"In a meeting with reporters at Scotland Yard, Miss Snyder's mother, Mrs. Maggie Snyder, said, 'Lily may have posed for artists, but she was a good girl. She never posed in the altogether.'"

"What does that mean?" asked Sara. "'In the altogether?'"

"Without any clothes on."

"That's what I thought," said Sara. She went on with the story:

"Mrs. Snyder was very critical of the police, saying, 'If Lily wasn't a working girl—if she came from Mayfair or Belgravia instead of Clerkenwell—the police would have stirred themselves a bit more to find her.' Inspector Finch, in charge of the case, denied this, saying, 'If she were a duchess's daughter we couldn't be trying harder to find her or discover what happened to her.'"

"What do you think happened to her?" asked Sara, putting down the paper. "Kidnapped by white slavers?"

"What do you know about white slavers?" asked Andrew.

"Probably more than you do. Don't forget I grew up in Dingell's Court, and we had some pretty rough judies around there."

"Yes, I know you did." He looked up as Matson came in and paused, waiting discreetly just inside the door. "Did you want me, Matson?"

"Yes, Master Andrew. Your mother wished me to request you to join her upstairs after you've finished your breakfast. She'd like you to come up too, Miss Sara."

"Thank you, Matson. We'll go right up." Matson bowed and withdrew. "I didn't think she was up yet. She doesn't usually get up this early, does she?"

"No," said Sara. "But someone came to see her a little while ago. A man from Hunt and Roskell."

"The jewelers?"

"I don't know. I just heard him say who he was to Matson before Matson took him up."

They went up the stairs to Verna's suite, which extended across the whole front of the house. As they reached the landing, the door of her sitting room opened and a dapper, middle-aged man in a morning coat came out.

"Then I shall see you tomorrow at about noon," he said to Verna.

"Yes, Mr. Jenkins. Thank you."

"No, Miss Tillett. Thank *you*."

He bowed to her, to Andrew and Sara and then went

down the stairs. Verna, wearing a pink silk robe with a marabou collar, was sitting at a small table near the window.

"Come in, you two," she said.

"Good morning, Mother," said Andrew. "I wasn't sure . . ." He broke off, staring, and Sara, standing next to him, gasped. There was a morocco jewel case on the table, and in front of it was a glittering mound of jewels.

"What's that?" asked Andrew.

"These?" said Verna. "They're what Mr. Jenkins brought." And she held up, first, a diamond and pearl tiara, then a diamond necklace with earrings to match.

"Are they real?" asked Sara.

"Yes, Sara. They're the Denham diamonds and quite famous."

"And you bought them?" said Andrew.

"Good heavens, no! They're not my style at all. Why would I want them?"

"Then I don't understand . . ."

"They're for the play. There's a scene where the young marquis insists that I try on the family jewels and, since Hunt and Roskell made the original settings for the Denham diamonds, Harrison had them make paste copies for me to use."

"But you said these were real," said Sara.

"They are. Harrison is giving a party at Claridge's to-night after the opening, and he thought, for an occasion like that, I should wear the originals rather than copies."

"But isn't it a little dangerous?" asked Andrew. "I mean, if anything happened to them . . ."

"I know. And I didn't like the idea, but Harrison insisted. He's taken out special insurance to cover them and also hired a detective to keep his eye on them at the theatre and afterwards at the party."

"And in the meantime?" asked Sara.

"In the meantime, as far as anyone except the two of you know, these are the copies that Mr. Jenkins brought me. I don't think we'll even tell your mother the truth, Sara, because it would worry her."

"It's worrying me," said Sara, her eyes large.

"Well, I refuse to let it worry me," said Verna. "If it's that important to Harrison, *he* can worry about it. But that's not why I asked the two of you to come up here. Did you have any plans for this afternoon?"

"Well, we had talked of going to the zoo," said Andrew. "Why?"

"You probably know what's happening next door, the marchioness's open house." Andrew nodded. "Well, I'm going, and I'd like the two of you to go with me."

"But that would be another quid apiece!" said Sara. Then, as Verna smiled, "I mean a pound."

"Well, it *is* for charity. I don't expect to stay long. I'll just stop in for a while before I go to the theatre, and you can either leave when I do or soon after."

"Of course, Mother," said Andrew. "What time did you plan to go?"

"About three thirty."

"Fine."

It was a little later than that before they were settled in the landau; Verna in a lavender taffeta dress, wearing a large straw hat and carrying a parasol, Sara in her white muslin, and Andrew in a dark blue jacket and trousers. Fred drove down the driveway, turned left on Rysdale Road and along it to the entrance to Three Oaks. There was a policeman at the gate, who saluted as they turned in. They drove through the landscaped grounds, past the small lake, the formal gardens and the terraces to the large and imposing Italianate house. There was another policeman under the porte-cochere and a footman in a white wig, knee-breeches and a tailcoat with brass buttons. When the landau stopped, he opened the door and helped Verna and Sara out. As Andrew got out, he saw that the policeman was Constable Wyatt, who looked at him impassively as policemen generally do, then spoiled the effect by winking.

Verna told Fred to come back for her at four thirty, and he touched his hat and drove off. As he did, a shiny double Victoria pulled in under the porte-cochere. Again the footman moved forward. Verna and Sara started into the house, and Andrew turned to smile at Wyatt before following them, then paused. The policeman had stiffened, color had come into his cheeks, and he was staring at the occupants of the carriage; a distinguished elderly gentleman with a bristling white mustache, a younger man in a military uniform and a young and attractive woman. The elderly man waved the footman aside impatiently, helped the young woman out of the carriage himself. Then he saw Wyatt.

"Good afternoon, sir," said Wyatt.

"You!" said the elderly man. He drew himself up, and his face flushed crimson. "How dare you address me?"

"I beg your pardon," said Wyatt, his face wooden. He stepped back, and the elderly man and the officer walked past him, but the woman paused.

"I don't know what to say, Peter," she said. "I wish—"

"Harriet!" said the officer.

"Yes, Francis," she said. She touched Wyatt lightly on the arm, then went after the two men.

Andrew followed them in. He found himself in an entrance hall with marble statues on two sides of it. At the far end was another footman, and standing next to him and waiting for Andrew were Verna and Sara. Murmuring an apology, Andrew brushed past the two men and the lady and joined Verna and Sara. To their left, at the entrance to a large salon, were two middle-aged and quite dissimilar ladies; one, in a long purple dress, was rather thin and blonde and had clearly been quite pretty once. The other was dark, taller and more vigorous looking.

"Miss Verna Tillett," announced the footman. "Miss Sara Wiggins. Master Andrew Tillett."

"You're my neighbor, are you not?" said the blonde lady, apparently the marchioness. "How nice of you to come. I've been most anxious to meet you."

"And I to meet you," said Verna.

"May I present my friend and house guest, Mrs. Van Gelder?" Then, to the tall, dark lady, "Miss Tillett is my nearest neighbor, and is also quite a well-known actress."

"Verna Tillett? I should say she is," said Mrs. Van Gelder with a decided American accent. "Weren't you in New York until about a year ago?"

"Yes, I was," said Verna.

"I remember seeing you in *The Dark Street*. I thought you were splendid."

"Thank you," said Verna.

The white-mustached, elderly man, the army officer and the attractive young woman were now approaching.

"General Wyatt," announced the footman. "Colonel and Mrs. Francis Wyatt."

"General," said the marchioness, extending a hand to the elderly man. "Delighted to see you again. You too, Colonel, and your lovely wife. May I present my friend and house guest, Mrs. Van Gelder, and my neighbor, Miss Verna Tillett?"

"How d'ya do?" said the general, nodding to Mrs. Van Gelder. Then, looking appreciatively at Verna, "Tillett. Familiar name. Related to Bobo Tillett of the Fusiliers?"

"I'm afraid not," said Verna with a smile. She introduced Sara and Andrew, and the general nodded to them, then turned his attention back to Verna.

"Hear there's champagne," he said. "Can I get you some?"

"That would be very kind of you," she said. Sara had curtsied to the marchioness, Mrs. Van Gelder, and then the general—another recently acquired social grace—and was now looking at the general with considerable interest. As she did, she tugged sharply at Andrew's jacket. Andrew looked at his mother and raised an inquiring eyebrow. She knew what he meant as he had known what Sara meant.

"Why don't the two of you look about by yourselves for a bit?" she said.

"If you don't mind, we will," said Andrew. He bowed to the marchioness, to the others, and he and Sara moved off into the salon.

"Did you get the general's name?" asked Sara.

"Wyatt. The same as the policeman's."

"Yes. They couldn't be related, could they?"

"Why not?"

"Because one's a general and the other's an ordinary bobby."

"It's still possible. They certainly know one another."

"How do you know?"

Andrew told her what had happened when the general arrived.

"Oh," said Sara. "Let's go find him—Constable Wyatt, I mean. You wanted to talk to him anyway, didn't you?"

They went out through one of the french doors and back to the porte-cochere. Carriages were still arriving, and though the footman was still there, Wyatt wasn't. They asked the footman where he was, and he told them Wyatt had gone down to relieve the constable at the gate.

"What do you want to do?" asked Andrew.

"See what's happening in those big tents," said Sara. "They're probably serving things in there. Then, after that, we can walk down through the grounds."

"Right."

They went down the steps of the terraces to one of the marquees and found that they were indeed serving things there. They had some tea sandwiches and small cakes, and though Sara looked longingly at the buffet, where liveried attendants were pouring champagne, Andrew said she was too young for it and she could have either tea or lemonade, and she settled for lemonade.

Afterwards they continued on down through the grounds, walking past the formal gardens and the lake. Near the lake was a grove of trees. In the middle of the grove, cut into the side of the hill and carefully land-scaped, was a dark and rocky opening. Andrew had seen grottoes before, but they were usually ornamental and shallow. This one, however, seemed quite deep and had a door closing it off. As he and Sara paused, looking at it, a sibilant voice said, "Sorry. No."

They turned and saw a strange-looking man sitting cross-legged in the shadow of a large oak. He was quite thin and dark. His head was shaved, and he wore a long, loose white robe.

"I beg your pardon?" said Andrew.

"This private, not open to public," he said with a curious, slurring accent.

"Oh. Sorry," said Andrew. To the left of the grove was a small, whitewashed cottage with a shingled roof.

"That private, too," said the man. "It where I live."

"I see," said Andrew. "Sorry if we disturbed you."

"Salaam," said the man. "The peace of Isis be with you."

"I wonder who he is," said Andrew as they walked away from him and down toward the gate.

"He has a funny name," said Sara. "Not Abraham. Ibrahim?"

"How do you know?"

"The marchioness's groom told Fred about him. About someone the marchioness brought back here from somewhere in the east. Could it be Egypt?"

"Isis was an Egyptian goddess," said Andrew. "But that was a long time ago. I didn't think anyone talked about her anymore." Then looking ahead, "There's Constable Wyatt."

He was standing just outside the gates, stopping pedestrians and traffic when a carriage arrived or left.

"Hello," he said. "Leaving already?"

"No," said Andrew. "Looking for you. Why are you down here instead of up at the house?"

"Finch pulled the other man off, so I had to take over on point duty."

"I see."

"Are you related to General Wyatt?" asked Sara.

Wyatt looked sharply at her, then at Andrew, and Andrew dropped his eyes. Though he had wondered about it too, having witnessed the exchange between the constable and the elderly man, he would never have asked that question.

"How do you know about General Wyatt?" he asked.

"He came in right after we did and we were introduced," said Sara.

"Oh. Yes, I'm related to him. He's my father."

"I knew you were a toff," said Sara. "But then why are you a copper?"

"That," said Wyatt, "seems to be a universal question, and one I've gotten a bit tired of answering."

"I guess I shouldn't have asked it then."

"I don't mind giving it another whirl. If your family had been Army for generations—if your father was a general, one brother a colonel and another a captain— wouldn't you be tempted to try something else?"

"Maybe. But why the police?"

"Why not? Is it more important—and more honorable —to fight Afghans, Abyssinians, Zulus and other spear-carrying natives than to fight against criminals here in London?"

"Well, no. But doesn't your family hate it?"

"Of course they do," said Andrew. "And that's the real reason he did it."

"What?" said Wyatt, turning toward him. "Why do you say that?"

"Sorry," said Andrew uncomfortably. "I shouldn't have."

"But you did. Now tell me why."

"I was there when your father and brother arrived and I saw how you looked at them and they looked at you."

"I see," said Wyatt. "I'm beginning to understand why Holmes said the things he did about you. It took me a little while to realize why I had done it myself."

"Become a policeman?"

"Yes. My father and I haven't always seen eye-to-eye, but I admire him. My brothers, on the other hand, are a pair of appalling snobs. They looked down their respective noses at me when I went to Cambridge instead of Sandhurst. And when they heard I was joining the Metropolitan Police, they became absolutely apoplectic. Which, as Holmes pointed out to me, was exactly what I wanted."

"But why aren't you at least a detective?" asked Sara.

"I must say you make a rare team," said Wyatt, smiling. "You ask the questions that Andrew is too much of a gentleman to ask—and he supplies the insights. Do you know how one becomes a detective in our Police Department as presently constituted?"

"No."

"After serving in the uniformed branch for two years —which I have done—a Divisional Detective Inspector can recommend that you be transferred to the C.I.D."

"Well?" said Sara.

"You mean, why haven't I been recommended?" asked Wyatt, still smiling. "I suppose you could say I haven't impressed anyone sufficiently with my intelligence, probity and reliability. But I'm not sure that's true because I've been noted and commended several times. I suspect that what I'm facing is the reverse of the attitude I face with my family. They're furious at me, consider me a traitor to my class because I'm a policeman . . . and the police dislike, distrust and resent me because I'm what you call a toff."

"Then you'd like to become a detective?" asked Andrew.

"Of course. Because, while I admit I liked the idea of thumbing my nose at my family, showing them up for a pack of snobs, that's the real reason I joined the police; because I wanted to become a detective."

"But you don't have to stay in the police to become one, do you?" asked Sara. "Mr. Holmes isn't in the police, doesn't even like them."

"That's true. And that's something he suggested too when I discussed the matter with him: that I quit and set up as a private investigator or consultant like him. However, there's a major difference between us: Holmes is a genius, and I'm not. And although I studied a great many things at Cambridge and after that I thought might be useful, I still felt I had a great deal to learn. And the place to learn was with the police."

"Well, maybe you'll still get your recommendation," said Andrew.

"Maybe. But I doubt it."

"How is Mr. Holmes, by the way?"

"He was quite well when I last saw him. But that was about a month ago. And of course, he's away now."

"Away?"

"Yes. He's on the continent somewhere. Even his friend, Dr. Watson, isn't sure where or how long he'll be gone."

"That's too bad. I was hoping to see him while I was in London and—"

He broke off as a four-wheeler came slowly down Rysdale Road. Inspector Finch, bowler hat tipped well forward, sat in the rear seat. Next to him was an elderly lady whose shawl was pulled up over her head so that you could barely see her tired, careworn face.

"Who's that in the carriage with Finch?" asked Sara.

"Mrs. Snyder, the mother of the girl who disappeared," said Wyatt. "She's been kicking up an awful row, claiming that if she had been West End instead of working class, the police would have done a lot more to find her daughter. So Finch has been taking her around himself to prove he's really working on the case."

"And hating it," said Andrew.

"Yes," said Wyatt. "Talk about snobs, he's one of the worst I've ever known, and . . . Here we go again," he said as the four-wheeler stopped and Finch beckoned to him. "Good-bye."

He went over to the four-wheeler, saluted Finch, took out his notebook and made some kind of report to him. Sara and Andrew watched him for a few minutes, then went back up through the grounds again to the house. When they arrived there, Fred was waiting and said he'd been about to come look for them because Miss Tillett wanted to leave. Then Verna came out and they went home together. Finch was gone, but Wyatt was still at the gate and he saluted them as they went by.

It was a little after five when they got to the house. Admitting that she was starting to feel tense, as she always did before an opening, Verna went up to her room to rest for a while. She came down again a little after six with Annie following her and carrying the Hunt and Roskell jewel case. The entire staff—the cook and kitchen maid as well as Matson, Mrs. Wiggins, Sara and Annie—

lined up outside to say good-bye to her as she got into the landau. They were all too aware of theatre tradition to wish her good luck—which could be almost as disastrous as whistling in the dressing room—but they listened attentively as Andrew asked her what time she thought she'd be home.

"Probably not until quite late," she said. "I don't expect to stay at the party for very long, but even then I don't imagine I'll be home before two or two thirty."

"I'll wait up for you," said Andrew.

"That's silly, darling."

"No, it's not. I want to hear all about it. If I'm not up, will you wake me?"

"Well, all right." She kissed him, waved to the others, then Fred shook the reins and they were off.

Not surprisingly, Verna came home later than she had expected. Andrew tried to wait up for her, as he had said he would, but he fell asleep around eleven o'clock, woke with a start when he heard carriage wheels on the gravel of the driveway. The book he had been reading had fallen to the floor, the gaslight over his head was still on, but he had no idea what time it was. He heard Matson open the downstairs door, and he got up, stepped into his slippers and went out into the hall. He glanced at the grandfather clock as he went by—it was ten after three—and he was standing at the top of the stairs when Verna came up them. She was wearing a long white evening gown and the Denham diamonds, and she looked magnificent; as regal as a duchess, but far more beautiful than any duchess had any need or right to look.

"Hello," said Andrew.

"Darling! You did wait up."

"Not really. I fell asleep, only woke up when you came home. How did it go?"

"Quite well."

"Just quite well?"

"Well, perhaps a bit better than that."

"Tell me."

"Get back into bed, and I'll come in. This tiara's starting to give a headache, and I want to take it off."

"Right."

He went back into his room, turned the light down slightly and got into bed. When Verna came in, he saw that she had taken off the earrings and necklace as well as the tiara, and he also saw that her eyes were bright with excitement.

"Well?" he said.

"It really did go quite well. There were two scenes Harrison was worried about—one with Fanny Farrell, who plays my mother, and the other with Rupert Trent, who plays the marquis. Well, Fanny was marvellous, had me in tears. As for Rupert, I thought he was still too extravagant, but he was definitely better."

"What about you? What did they think of you?"

She shrugged. "How can you tell? I had six curtain

calls, but I don't think that meant anything. This was opening night, I haven't played a dramatic role here in years and I think everyone was determined to be kind."

"But didn't anyone *say* anything?"

"Well, Harrison did—he said I was splendid. And so did William Archer and most of the theatre people who were at the Claridge. But there again, it was an opening night party and one's expected to be enthusiastic. Let's wait and see what the critics say tomorrow."

"Isn't Mr. Archer a critic?"

"Yes. But what he said to me and what he'll say in the paper can be two very different things."

"What about Mr. Shaw? Was he at the party?"

"Yes, he was. He didn't stay very long, but . . . All right. He said he wasn't going to spend much time discussing the play—which was just about what he had thought it would be—but that, while he had expected a great deal of my performance, he found he had grossly underestimated me."

"Well, there you are, then."

"Oh, I admit that I was pleased—by that and by what everyone else said—and I suspect that the play will do very well."

"I'm sure it will. And so is Fred."

"Fred?"

"He said he's talked to the stagehands and the man at the stage door and they think you're wonderful and that the play's going to be a tremendous hit."

"Then I certainly needn't worry," she said laughing. She stifled a yawn. "I'm suddenly very tired. Will you tell Mrs. Wiggins to see that no one wakes me tomorrow? I'll get up when I get up."

"Yes, Mother."

"Good night, darling. It's very nice to have you here to talk to when I get home."

"I like it too."

"Good." She bent down and kissed him. "See you in the morning."

"Yes, Mother."

She turned out the light and went out, closing the door behind her. Smiling, he closed his eyes, preparing to go back to sleep, then sat up as his mother cried out. Throwing off the covers, he ran across the hall. The door of Verna's dressing room was open and she was standing just inside it, staring at her dressing table.

"Mother, what is it?" he asked.

She pointed to the jewel box, which was open and empty.

"The diamonds," she said. "The Denham diamonds. I left them here when I took them off—and now they're gone!"

4

Inspector Finch

Andrew's problem the next morning was not to see that his mother was not disturbed, but to persuade her to get some rest. Immediately after they discovered that the diamonds were missing, they sent Fred for the police. When he returned, he told them that there was only a sergeant on duty at the Wellington Road police station, but that a detective would be around to the house the first thing in the morning.

The detective turned out to be Inspector Finch, and he arrived, not the first thing in the morning, but about ten o'clock. On the positive side, however—at least as far as Andrew was concerned—the constable with him was Wyatt. Matson had shown them into the front sitting room, and Finch frowned slightly as Andrew came in.

"Good morning," he said. "You're Andrew Tillett?"

"Yes."

"I'm Inspector Finch. I understand your mother's still asleep."

"Not asleep, resting. She only got to bed about five thirty. But she's been told that you're here, and she should be down shortly."

"Good. She's Verna Tillett, the actress?"

"Yes."

"I don't suppose you can tell me the circumstances of the robbery."

"Yes, I can. She was with me when it took place."

"And you know what was stolen?"

"Yes."

"Well, perhaps it might save time if you told us about it while we're waiting for her. Constable, take notes."

"Yes, Inspector," said Wyatt. Standing behind the inspector, he produced a notebook and pencil.

"Wouldn't it be easier if you sat down, Constable?" asked Andrew.

"Thank you, sir. I'm all right."

"Of course, he's all right," said Finch. "Let's get on with it."

As succinctly as he could, Andrew told him everything he knew about the robbery.

"You're sure about the time?" asked Finch.

"Yes, Inspector. I told you I looked at the clock when I heard my mother come home."

"And she was with you for how long?"

"You mean before she discovered that the jewels were gone? Not more than ten minutes."

"Hmm. Will you come outside with us, show us just where her room is?"

"Yes, Inspector."

Sara had waited outside when Andrew went in to talk to the inspector. Now, seeing her sitting at the foot of the stairs, Finch said, "Who's this?"

"Sara Wiggins," said Andrew.

"She lives here?"

"Of course," said Andrew. More and more irritated by Finch's manner, he said to Sara, "We're going outside so I can show the inspector where mother's room is. Come on along with us."

Sara stood up. Finch looked as if he were trying to think of some reason why she shouldn't come, but apparently he wasn't able to. Matson opened the door, and they went out, down the two steps from the porte-cochere and across the driveway to the front lawn. They turned, looking back at the house, and Andrew pointed up to a corner window.

"That's one of the windows of her dressing room," he said. "There's another just around the corner. The other windows on the front are her bedroom."

Finch and Wyatt studied the facade of the house. The windows were between twenty and twenty-five feet from the ground. There was nothing near them up which anyone could have climbed—a drain pipe, wisteria or even ivy—and the freshly painted stucco offered no hand or footholds. Above the front windows—and just under those on the third floor—were a pair of small, ornamental iron balconies.

"Whose room is that?" asked Finch, pointing to the third floor.

"I'm not sure," said Andrew. He looked at Sara. "Matson's?"

She nodded.

"That's the butler?"

"Yes."

"Let's go back in."

He led the way, Sara and Andrew followed him and Wyatt came last. As Finch started up the steps, he glanced back. Wyatt, lagging behind, was studying the ground near the corner of the house.

"What are you doing, Wyatt?" he asked.

"Nothing, sir."

"No? Then come along."

"Yes, sir," said Wyatt, his face expressionless.

As they entered the house, Matson was coming down the stairs.

"Miss Tillett thought you would like to see the room from which the jewels were stolen," he said. "She suggested, therefore, that I bring you upstairs."

"Very good," said Finch. "Very intelligent of her."

Gravely, Matson went back upstairs, knocked at the door of Verna's dressing room and, when she responded, opened it and announced Finch. Verna, wearing a blouse and skirt and looking pale and upset, held out her hand.

"Sorry that it is under such unfortunate circumstances," said Finch bowing over it, "but still delighted to make your acquaintance."

"You're very kind," she said. She looked at Wyatt, who had taken off his helmet and was standing at the door with it under his arm. "And who is your colleague?"

"Hmm? Oh, he's not my colleague. That's just Constable Wyatt. May I look around?"

"That's why I suggested you come up here."

She watched as he went to the window, looked out, then examined the jewel case on the dressing table.

"The diamonds were in here?"

"Yes."

"Was it locked?"

"No. I merely dropped the diamonds into it when I went into my son's room. I wasn't in there more than ten minutes."

"So your son said. He also said that the diamonds were not yours."

"No. They were lent to me by Hunt and Roskell, who had made the copies of them for me to wear in the play."

"How many people knew that the diamonds you wore last night were real, not copies?"

"Well, Mr. Jenkins of Hunt and Roskell. And Mr. Harrison, the theatre manager, who had arranged for it . . ."

"I meant, how many people here in the house?"

"Only my son and Sara."

"Sara?"

"Sara Wiggins, my housekeeper's daughter."

"Oh," Finch turned and looked at Sara, who stood in the doorway next to Andrew. "Your son said she lived here, but he didn't say who she was. Your butler didn't know?"

"No. I told you, only Sara and my son. I didn't even want Mrs. Wiggins to know because I was afraid it would worry her."

"Why would it worry her?"

"Because she's that kind of person. She worries about anything that concerns me or the house."

"I see. I'd like to talk to her, to the other members of your staff. May I?"

"I suppose so. But why?"

"They may have seen or heard something."

"If they had, they would have told me, but go ahead."

"Thank you." He bowed to her, jerked his head at Wyatt and went out. Wyatt followed, and, after a glance at Andrew, Sara followed Wyatt.

"I wish you weren't so upset about this," said Andrew.

"So do I."

"But you said you weren't going to worry about the stupid diamonds. You said you didn't want to wear them or even have them here."

"I know. But once I agreed to, it seems to me I accepted responsibility for them. I shouldn't have left them alone."

"For ten minutes in your own home?"

"It does seem odd, doesn't it?"

"Very." He looked at the chair next to her dressing table. "Is that today's paper?"

"Yes. Matson brought it up just a few minutes ago."

"Is there a review of the play in it?"

"Yes."

"Good?"

"Quite good." She handed him the paper. It was open to the review, and he read it quickly. To say it was good was an understatement. It was extremely enthusiastic, particularly about her performance.

The play is well made and would probably be dramatic and moving no matter how it was cast," said the last paragraph. "But with Miss Verna Tillett playing the squire's daughter it becomes an unforgettable experience. We are, of course, familiar with Miss Tillett's comic gifts, but we are in Mr. Harrison's debt for giving us an opportunity to see her in a dramatic role in which she gives one of the most brilliant performances it has been our pleasure to witness in many years.

"But that's wonderful, mother!"

"I'm pleased with it. Now if the others are anything like that . . ."

"They will be, won't they?"

"I suspect so. Walker is the most austere critic in London, and if he liked it, I'm fairly sure the others will."

"I'm glad. I know you've been anxious about it."

"Yes, I was. And I'd be very happy today if it wasn't for this other thing—the robbery."

"I know. Are you coming downstairs?"

"You mean while the inspector questions the staff? No. He's wasting his time and theirs. I spoke to them myself, and none of them knows anything about what happened. They were all asleep except Matson, and he had just gone up to his room."

"I imagine the inspector has got to question everyone. Do you mind if I go down?"

"No. But I can't think why . . ." Then, with a smile, "How silly of me. Of course you'd be interested. Not that the inspector is a Sherlock Holmes."

"No, he isn't. But I'd still like to see how he goes about things."

"Naturally. Well, run along, darling, and perhaps I'll come down later."

What Verna didn't seem to realize was that even though Holmes had nothing to do with the case, it was just as interesting to Andrew as the previous one, since the crime had not only taken place in his own house but had involved jewels for which his mother felt responsible.

When Andrew got downstairs, he found Sara on the

bench outside the sitting room. Finch had left the door open and glancing inside, Andrew saw Wyatt sitting at a boule table, taking notes.

"Matson's in there with him," whispered Sara, making room for him. "He's just started talking to him."

"How long have you been here?" asked Finch.

"About eight months," said Matson.

"And where were you before that?"

"Lord Gower's in Montrose Place. I was his butler for fourteen years—until he died last September."

"Was this the Lord Gower whose horse won the Derby two years ago?"

"Yes, sir."

"Oh, well," said Finch as if that settled that. "Will you tell me again what you remember of last night?"

"Yes, Inspector. As I told you, Miss Tillett came home at a little after three. I let her in, and she went up to her room . . ."

"She was wearing the jewels at the time?"

"Yes, inspector. A tiara, diamond necklace and earrings. I locked up—"

"When you say you locked up, you mean you locked the front door, don't you?"

"Yes, Inspector. I had already locked the rear door and made certain of the windows. Then I went up to my room. As I went past Mr. Andrew's room, I saw that the light was on and heard voices so I knew Miss Tillett was in there, talking to him. I reached my room and had just taken off my jacket when I heard Miss Tillett cry out. I hurried down to her room, and she told me that the jewels had been stolen."

"You saw or heard nothing else between the time Miss Tillett went upstairs and the time she cried out?"

"No, Inspector."

"Well, that's all very clear. Thank you. Now will you send in the housekeeper . . . What's her name—Wiggins?"

"Yes, Inspector."

Matson came out and went to the breakfast room where the rest of the staff was waiting. Meanwhile Finch walked over to Wyatt.

"Are you getting all this?" he asked.

"Yes, Inspector."

"Let's see." He picked up Wyatt's notebook, then scowled. "What's all this? I can't read a word of it!"

"It's in shorthand."

"Why?"

"When I use it, I can get things down more quickly."

"And what if something happened to you? Who could read it?"

"Anyone who can read shorthand."

"Well, from now on you take in your notes in ordinary writing. I—" He broke off as Mrs. Wiggins came in. "Mrs. Wiggins?"

"Yes, Inspector."

"Your full name, please."

"Mrs. Harold Wiggins."

"Your marital status?"

"Widow."

"Sit down, Mrs. Wiggins." Andrew and Sara could no longer see her, but they heard the scrape of a chair as she sat down. "How long have you been working here?"

"About nine months, since immediately after Miss Tillett bought this house."

"And where were you before that?"

"You mean where did I live or where did I work?"

"Both."

"I lived in Dingell's Court near Edgeware Road and I worked in several places. You see, I used to do charring and—"

"Charring? But you're the housekeeper here, aren't you?"

"Yes."

"Why did Miss Tillett engage you as housekeeper when you'd had no previous experience?"

"I think it was because of Master Andrew."

"What do you mean?"

"About a year ago, when Miss Tillett was away in America, Master Andrew was brought to London by his tutor. The tutor disappeared and left him completely alone, not knowing a soul except my daughter, Sara."

"How did he know her?"

"He'd met her on Baker Street, near Mr. Holmes's

rooms. A day or so later he was robbed, hurt. My son Sam brought him to our place, and he lived with us until his mother found him. She was grateful to us for taking care of him and when she bought the house she offered me the job of housekeeper and I took it."

"I see. Will you tell me what you did after supper last night?"

"I didn't do very much. Sara and Andrew played parcheesi for a while, and I did my accounts and watched them. At a little before ten we all went upstairs. I fell asleep almost immediately and only woke up when Miss Tillett called out."

"Where is your room?"

"On the second floor, near the back."

"The same floor as Miss Tillett's?"

"Yes."

"When did you first hear about the diamonds?"

"Hear about them?"

"Hear that they were real."

"When Miss Tillett cried out and I went into her room."

"You didn't know it before that?"

"No. During lunch Mr. Matson said that a man from Hunt and Roskell had been here and brought Miss Tillett some paste jewelry she was going to wear in the play."

"Odd you didn't know that the diamonds were real. Your daughter knew."

"She told me that later on, but she said Miss Tillett hadn't wanted me to know because she was afraid it would worry me."

"And would it have worried you?"

"Of course. But I would rather have worried than feel as awful as I do now"

"Why do you feel awful?"

"Because it's a terrible thing to have had happen, and in a way, I guess I feel responsible."

"You do?"

"Of course. After all, I am the housekeeper and Mr. Matson and I are responsible for everything that happens here."

"I see. How much do you think the diamonds are worth?"

"I've no idea."

"You must have some idea."

"I haven't. I never even saw them, just the case they were in."

"What would you say if I told you they were worth about forty thousand pounds? At least, that's what they're insured for."

"Forty thousand . . . ?"

"Yes. They are, of course, extremely well known and as soon as I get back to the Yard word will go out to every dealer in England, America and the continent informing them that they've been stolen. So how do you expect to get rid of them?"

"How do I . . . ?"

"Yes. Who do you think will buy them from you, take them off your hands?"

Somehow Sara had sensed where Finch's questions were tending before Andrew did, and she had stiffened and begun frowning. At this last one, she leaped to her feet and started toward the sitting room. But someone else was before her. Verna had come down the stairs, and, waving Sara aside, went in ahead of her.

"All right, Inspector," she said with icy finality. "That's enough."

Sara and Andrew had followed Verna in. Mrs. Wiggins had risen and was standing there with a look of shocked horror on her face, and Sara went over to her and took her hand. Finch, meanwhile, had turned to Verna with mild surprise.

"I beg your pardon?" he said.

"It is Mrs. Wiggins' pardon you should be begging, not mine. For what you're suggesting is that she took the diamonds!"

"That's right."

"You mean you admit it? How dare you make such an outrageous accusation?"

"I'm sorry, Miss Tillett. I know it always comes as a bit of a surprise, but I've had a good bit of experience in cases of this sort and I ask you to look at the facts. Robberies are either inside jobs or outside jobs, right?"

"Well?"

"Well, having ascertained the circumstances of the crime, I examined the premises and immediately saw that there was no way anyone could climb up to your window and enter. In other words, it couldn't be an outside job. Which means it had to be an inside job."

"Which in turn meant that Mrs. Wiggins was the thief, is that correct?"

"Well, it stands to reason, doesn't it? It couldn't be your butler—he was with Lord Gower for fourteen years. But Mrs. Wiggins was just a charlady before she came here, and I'll wager you never even asked for her references."

"No, I didn't."

"Well, there you are. No references, knew about the diamonds—at least her daughter did. Doesn't that make her a logical suspect? Of course, it might be someone else on your staff—the upstairs maid or the cook or the tweeny—and I'll get to them, question them. But in the meantime—"

"Just a second, Inspector. Am I to understand that, having accused Mrs. Wiggins of having stolen the diamonds, you now intend to accuse everyone else in the house of the same crime?"

"Yes, Miss Tillett. That way we can see who the most likely suspect is. It's fairly standard procedure—"

"Well, it's not going to be used here. I think you'd better go, Inspector!"

"I don't understand—"

"That's obvious! I have complete faith in everyone in this house but particularly in Mrs. Wiggins, and I don't intend to have any of them bothered, badgered or exposed to your ridiculous questions. So, as I said, I think you'd better go."

"I'd like to remind you," said Finch, drawing himself up, "that a crime has been committed—"

"I agree!" said Verna, her eyes blazing. "Your accusation was a crime against my intelligence and against generally accepted civilized behavior, and I will not tolerate it! That is why I insist that you leave."

"Very well," said Finch, his face flushed. "But I must warn you that this is not the end. You can't trifle with the police this way. I'll be back." And jerking his head at Wyatt, he stalked out of the room. Wyatt closed his notebook and stood up, looking at Verna with frank admiration.

"Wyatt!" called Finch from outside.

"Coming, Inspector," he said. Bowing to Verna, he followed Finch to the door and they both left. Still looking stricken, Mrs. Wiggins watched them go. Then, turning to Verna, she tried to say something, couldn't, burst into tears and ran out of the room. Sara followed her.

"Well, this is a fine thing!" said Verna, still indignant. "And it certainly hasn't increased my respect for Scotland Yard. Do you think your friend, Mr. Holmes, would have approached the case this way?"

"No," said Andrew.

"Neither do I. Excuse me." And she went off after Mrs. Wiggins, too. Andrew went to the window and looked out. Finch and Wyatt were walking down the driveway together. When they reached Rysdale Road, Finch, scowling, said something to Wyatt. Wyatt saluted, Finch went off and Wyatt began walking slowly up and down the hedge that separated the garden from the street. He was still there a few minutes later when Sara came back into the sitting room.

"Is she all right now?" asked Andrew.

"Yes," said Sara. "What are you looking at?"

"Constable Wyatt. He seems to be staying here."

Sara looked out of the window, then at Andrew. Without a word they went out and down the driveway to the street.

"Hello," said Andrew.

"Hello," said Wyatt. "I was hoping you'd come out. I wanted to apologize to you for Finch's behavior."

"That's all right. We know you didn't think Mrs. Wiggins had anything to do with it."

"No, I didn't."

"Why are you staying here?" asked Sara.

"Finch's orders. He's still angry, wants me to watch the house, tell him who goes in and out."

"Why?" asked Andrew. "Does he think that whoever stole the diamonds may come out and wave them under your nose?"

"Maybe," said Wyatt with a grin.

"Do you have any idea who could have taken them?" asked Sara. "And how?"

"You need facts before you can even begin to develop a theory, and I don't have any. You heard Finch when I tried to look around."

"Yes," said Andrew. "Why don't you come in and look around now?"

"I can't. Finch is perfectly capable of coming back to see if I'm obeying orders and staying on my post out here."

"Couldn't we do it for you?" asked Sara. "Look around, I mean."

"I've been thinking about that. It wouldn't do any harm."

"Where do you want us to look?" asked Andrew. "And for what?"

"I can tell you where to look, but that's all. There are flower beds under the two dressing room windows. Go over them carefully and tell me what you find there. Then go upstairs and examine the sills of the dressing room windows."

"All right," said Andrew. "We'll be back in a little while."

In order to save time, they decided to split up and Andrew searched the flower beds while Sara went inside and up to the dressing room. Both Holmes and Wyatt had complimented Andrew on the way he used his eyes and he tried to be particularly careful now, going over both beds inch by inch. He was still looking when Sara came out.

"Find anything?" she asked.

"I'm not sure. Maybe."

"What did you find?"

"Let's go back and talk to Wyatt."

The constable had walked up the street toward Three Oaks while he was waiting, but when he saw them he came hurrying back.

"Well?" he said.

"I did the flower beds," said Andrew. "There was nothing in the one around the side of the house, but there were some faint marks on the edge of the grass near the bed in front of the house that might have been footprints."

"Oh? Nothing in the bed itself?"

"A few little white flakes of something. Here." He gave Wyatt a fragment that was half the size of his smallest finger nail. Wyatt studied it, then rubbed it between his fingers and it crumbled.

"What do you think it is?" he asked.

"A bit of stucco," said Andrew.

"That's what I think too. What about the sills of the dressing room windows?"

"I did those," said Sara. "There was nothing on the one to the side, but there was a little smear of dirt in the middle of the one in front."

"When you say dirt," said Wyatt, "do you mean dust or do you mean earth, garden dirt?"

"I mean garden dirt," said Sara. "I couldn't blow it away, and when I rubbed it, it smeared."

"I said you two make quite a team," said Wyatt. "And you do."

"Thanks," said Andrew. "If I'm following you, you don't think it was an inside job. You think someone came in through the window."

"That's right."

"But how could they without a ladder—and a very long ladder at that? And if they did use a ladder wouldn't Matson, Mother or I have heard them?"

"Probably. But I don't think they did use a ladder."

"How did they get up to the window then?"

"I'd rather not say—not quite yet."

5

The Second Robbery

It was Fred who brought them word of the next robbery. When Andrew came downstairs the next morning,
Fred, his eyes bright with excitement, was talking to Sara
outside the breakfast room. Seeing Andrew, Sara checked
Fred and said, "Tell him."

"Oh, he wouldn't be interested," said Fred, looking at
Andrew.

"Stop teasing and tell him."

"All right. Well, mate, seems like we're not the only
pebble on the beach or the only pigeon in St. John's
Wood either."

"What do you mean?"

"There's been another robbery, right next door at the
marchioness's."

"What? How do you know?"

"How do you think I know? Because I did it."

"Come on, Fred. Tell me."

"Well, use your loaf. When you get robbed, you send for the police. Who do you send? A coachman, a groom or a stableboy. I'm up early exercising the new hunter when who comes down the road but young Billy from next door riding the gelding I'll be borrowing for you. I ask him what's up and he tells me."

"Who was robbed? The marchioness?"

"No. Her American friend, Mrs. Van Gelder."

"Did she lose very much?"

"Billy said from the way she was taking on you'd think it was the crown jewels, but of course, that don't mean nothing."

"No, I don't suppose it does. I wonder if Inspector Finch will be handling that case, too."

"He will."

"How do you know *that?*"

"Because the sergeant at the police station said that one of Scotland Yard's best men was working on *our* robbery and that he'd be over to see the marchioness as soon as he got in."

"That does sound like Finch—though if he's Scotland Yard's best, we're in a bad way. Could you keep your eye on the road and let us know when he gets there?"

"Why do you want to know that?"

"I'd just like to."

7 *1*

"You're up to something, I'm not sure what. All right. I'll let you know." And he went off.

"Have you had breakfast?" Andrew asked Sara.

"I always have it with Mum, but I'll come in and sit with you." She waited until he'd helped himself from the dishes on the buffet, then said, "Well?"

"There's something strange about this. First mother's robbed, then someone right next door is."

"You think it was the same person—or the same gang?"

"I don't know, but wouldn't you like to go over to Three Oaks and find out just how it was done, see if it's anything like the way mother was robbed?"

"Of course, I would, but how can we? Even if they let us in—and they probably wouldn't—nobody would talk to us."

"No, but they would talk to Mother."

"Oh. Do you think she'd do it—go over there and let us come with her?"

"I'll ask her and see. Is she up yet?"

"I don't think so. And she probably won't be for a while—not after yesterday."

The day before had been very difficult. Shortly after Finch left, Mr. Harrison, the theatre manager, had arrived. With the help of Wyatt and the constable who replaced him later, he kept the newspaper men who gathered outside the house away from Verna, and he remained with her while she discussed the robbery with

Mr. Jenkins of Hunt and Roskell and then with the man from the insurance company. By then it was time to leave for the theatre for the matinee, and she had stayed there until after the evening performance.

"Well, will you ask Annie to call us as soon as she does get up?"

"All right. In the meantime, read that." And she nodded at the morning paper, which lay on the table. It wasn't as neatly folded as usual, and he suspected that for once Sara had read it before he had.

He picked it up as she went upstairs and had no trouble finding the story. It was near the bottom of the front page and was captioned: ROBBERY IN ST. JOHN'S WOOD. It mentioned the play and discussed Verna's career and the history of the Denham diamonds, but it did not tell Andrew anything about the robbery that he did not know already except for the ending, which stated that Inspector Finch of Scotland Yard, who was in charge of the case, had several leads and expected to make an arrest very shortly.

Andrew had just finished reading the article when Sara came back into the breakfast room.

"Annie says she's up. She rang for her breakfast tray a little while ago."

"Let's us go up then."

Verna was sitting up in bed, drinking her tea and reading the paper that Annie had brought up with the tray.

"I didn't think you'd be up yet, Mother," said Andrew.

"Neither did I, but there it is." She held up her copy of the paper. "Did you read this?"

"Yes."

"Is that what you wanted to talk to me about?"

"No. There's something we wanted to tell you. There was another robbery last night—right next door."

"What? You mean the marchioness was robbed?"

"No. Her friend, Mrs. Van Gelder."

"What did she lose—money, jewels?"

"Fred thinks jewels."

"Oh. You know, in a curious way, that makes me feel better. I mean, if a gang's operating out here—if they robbed her as well as me—I don't feel quite as guilty about the Denham diamonds. Don't you think there may be some connection between the two robberies?"

"Yes, we do," said Andrew.

Verna looked at him, at Sara, then at him again.

"All right," she said. "What is it? You didn't come up here just to tell me about the robbery."

"Yes, we did. We thought . . . Well, don't you think it would be neighborly for you to go over there and tell the marchioness how sorry you are?"

"What? But I hardly know her. I just met her once, when we were over there at her open house."

"But you *are* her neighbor, and you were just robbed too," said Sara. "Don't you think she'd like to hear how it happened and tell you how it happened to Mrs. Van Gelder?"

Verna looked at them again.

"I see," she said. "Meaning *you'd* like to hear how it happened."

"Well, if you did go," said Andrew, "we'd like to come along. Nobody paid any attention to us the last time we went over there, and I don't think they would this time, either."

"You really do have it quite bad, don't you?"

"What?"

"The itch to play detective. I'm not sure I approve. It was one thing when you were working with Mr. Holmes. It's another to try to do it on your own."

"But we wouldn't do it on our own."

"No? Who did you plan to work with—Finch?"

"No. We're as convinced he's a fool as you are. But Constable Wyatt isn't."

"Constable Wyatt?"

"He's General Wyatt's son," said Sara. "And he knows Mr. Holmes too, and he became a policeman because he doesn't want to be a soldier like his father and brothers. And what he'd really like is to become a detective, but Finch won't recommend him for it because he's jealous of him."

"How do you know so much about him?"

"We've been talking to him," said Andrew. "He's

very nice and very intelligent, and he thinks he has some idea of how the diamonds were stolen."

"I see. Apparently quite a bit's been going on that I didn't know about. Do you think Finch will be looking into the robbery at the marchioness's?"

"Yes, we do. And we hope Constable Wyatt will be in on it, too."

"I'm beginning to understand why you're so anxious to have me go over there. And I suppose, if we do go, it had better be soon."

"The sooner the better."

"All right," said Verna, throwing back the covers. "Tell Fred to bring the carriage round. I'll be down in ten minutes."

"Mother," said Andrew, "you're ream!"

"I'm glad you think so," she said, disappearing into her dressing room.

Only an actress, accustomed to quick changes, could have gotten ready in that time and done it with no signs of haste.

"Good morning, ma'am," said Fred, opening the door of the landau. Then to Andrew, "The Yard bird's next door."

"Finch?"

"Isn't that the one you asked me to watch out for?"

"Yes. Thanks, Fred." He turned to Verna. "I thought we'd get there before he did. Are you going to mind, Mother?"

"Not really. If he's there, a different kind of performance will be called for, but that's all."

Like all her performances, this one was extremely effective. Arriving at Three Oaks, she swept regally past the footman and the policeman at the door and, with Sara and Andrew following closely behind her, marched into the salon. The marchioness, wearing a dressing gown and looking haggard, was there. Mrs. Van Gelder, also in a dressing gown, was with her and so were Finch and Constable Wyatt.

"I just heard the news," said Verna, ignoring everyone but the marchioness, "and I had to come over and tell you how sorry I was."

"That's very kind of you."

"It's not kind at all. After all, I've just been through the same thing and—" She hesitated as if she had first become aware of the others. "Oh. I hope I haven't come at a bad time."

"Not at all. This is Inspector Finch of Scotland Yard. He just arrived and—"

"I know the inspector. He's been investigating my robbery, and you couldn't have anyone better looking into the one that took place here."

"Nice of you to say so," muttered Finch awkwardly. "Still haven't really gotten anywhere there . . ."

"But I'm sure that now you will," said Verna. Then to Mrs. Van Gelder. "It was your jewels that were taken?"

"Yes. They may not have been as costly and famous as the Denham diamonds, but they meant a great deal to me. There was a string of Cartier pearls that Mr. Van Gelder gave me for our tenth anniversary, an emerald and diamond brooch and matching emerald ring—"

"You've already given us a list of the articles that were stolen," said Finch. "Now I'd like you to tell me just when and how the robbery took place."

"It took place last night, sometime between two and six in the morning."

"You're sure about the time?"

"Yes. The marchioness and I went out to a concert at the Queen's Hall and then to a reception at Lord Burdett's. We got home after one. I was wearing the jewels, as the marchioness and half of London can testify, and only took them off when I retired, which was about two o'clock. They were gone when I woke this morning."

"They were taken from your room?"

"Yes. From the dressing table."

"Was the door of your room open or locked?"

"Locked."

"Indeed it was," said the marchioness. "We got into the habit of locking our doors when we were in the east, and even though I haven't thought it was necessary, Mrs. Van Gelder has continued to do so here. As a matter of fact, when I wanted to get into her room this morning, I couldn't for some time because the lock had jammed and she couldn't turn the key."

"How extraordinary!" said Verna. "The Denham diamonds were taken from my room too, but the door was open. Does that mean that in this case someone came in from the outside and took them?"

"I won't know that until I've examined the scene of the crime," said Finch. "May I?" he asked Mrs. Van Gelder.

"Of course. This way," and she led the inspector and Wyatt off. Verna glanced after them, apparently deciding that even she couldn't go with them without an invitation, and continued to talk to the marchioness, commiserating with her and asking her if she were prepared for an assault by the press.

"Do you think they'll come round here?"

"I think it's very likely. There were about a dozen reporters over at my house yesterday afternoon."

"I'll leave word that they're not to be allowed in," said the marchioness. She went to the door of the salon and tugged at a bell pull. When her butler appeared, the policeman who had been outside was with him. They talked for a moment, then the policeman went off with the butler, and the marchioness returned to Verna.

"I gave instructions about the press," she said. "But there's something else. That policeman said he had an urgent message for Inspector Finch. I wonder what it was."

"Perhaps he'll tell us when he comes down," said Verna.

"Perhaps," said the marchioness, and she began to tell Verna how awful she felt about the robbery. "Almost as if," she said, "it were my fault."

"That's ridiculous!" said Verna. "Why is it your fault?"

"Because it happened while Mrs. Van Gelder was staying here in my house."

"But it could have happened no matter where she was staying. Didn't you say you had gotten into the habit of locking your doors when you were in the east?"

"Yes. We were told to do so for fear of theft when we were in Egypt. But—" She broke off as Finch came into the room, followed by Wyatt and Mrs. Van Gelder.

"I hope you'll forgive me, ma'am," said Finch, a strained and worried look on his face, "but I just received an urgent message from the Yard, and I'm afraid I have to leave."

"Leave?" said the marchioness. "But what about Mrs. Van Gelder's jewels?"

"I've looked over her room, made some notes, and I'm leaving Constable Wyatt here to make further notes, which I'll go over this afternoon. Obviously I've only begun work on the case—as I have on the theft of the Denham diamonds—but I hope to have something to report to you within a day or so."

"I sincerely hope so," said the marchioness.

"So do I," said Verna. She watched Finch leave, then said, "I think I'll go, too. But I believe you'll find Constable Wyatt every bit as competent as Inspector Finch."

"I'm delighted to hear that," said the marchioness. She turned to Wyatt. "Is there anything more you want to ask us?"

"No, ma'am," he said, bowing politely. "I'd like to look over the grounds now if I may."

"By all means. Go anywhere you like and look at anything you like."

"Thank you, ma'am," he said, bowing again. He waited while Verna said good-bye, then fell in behind Sara and Andrew as they all went out.

"I hope you'll forgive me for comparing you to Finch," said Verna.

"Knowing how you feel about him, I did not take it as a compliment," said Wyatt. "Apart from that, however, may I consider it an expression of confidence?"

"You may."

"In that case, since we haven't talked before, I know who's responsible. Thank you," he said to Sara and Andrew.

"You're welcome," said Sara.

"They, of course, are the reason I came over here," said Verna.

"I gathered that. And I can't tell you how much I admired the way you handled it."

"Well, they were very anxious to find out what was going on. But what happens now is up to you. If you think they'll be in your way, I'll take them home."

"They won't be in my way. They were very helpful yesterday."

"Oh? Well, I'm not surprised. I'll run along then. Good-bye, darlings."

They said good-bye and watched her drive off in the landau.

"Your mother," said Wyatt, "is quite an extraordinary person. I thought so yesterday, and I'm more convinced of it than ever now."

"Yes, she is," said Andrew. "You didn't mind our coming over then?"

"No."

"Good," said Sara. "Then tell us what that urgent message was, why Finch had to leave."

"I don't see what they have to do with one another," said Wyatt with a smile. "But I'll tell you anyway. There's been another jewel robbery."

"You mean besides ours and this one?"

"Yes. This wasn't in St. John's Wood. It was in Mayfair—South Audley Street. But the person who was robbed, Lady Damien, is a friend of the commissioner."

"That's why Finch left in such a hurry," said Andrew. "And also why he looked so upset."

"Three robberies in three days," said Wyatt, nodding. "The first two, at least, important ones, and so far no real clues."

"None here either?" asked Sara.

"Not that I've come across so far. Apparently the door was locked."

"What about the windows?" asked Andrew.

"They were open, but they didn't seem any more accessible than the ones in your mother's dressing room. At least, from the inside. I was just going to look at them from the outside."

"Can we go with you?" asked Sara.

"Of course. This way."

They went down off the porte-cochere and around the side of the house.

"Those are her windows," said Wyatt, pointing.

They were, as he had said, even more inaccessible than the windows of Verna's dressing room; at least thirty-five feet from the ground, with nothing that could be climbed on either side, above or below them. Wyatt shook his head.

"Better stay where you are till I've had a look," he said, going closer to the face of the house. They watched as he examined the flower bed below the windows, then moved further away, studying the grass of the lawn.

"Anything?" asked Andrew.

"No. At least not that I could see." He straightened up, looked at the terraces and the formal gardens, then down past them at the grove of trees and the white-washed cottage. "What's down there?" he asked.

"There's kind of a cave where those trees are," said

Sara. "And a man with a strange name lives in the cottage."

"What name?"

"Sara thinks it's Ibrahim," said Andrew. "He might be Egyptian—he looks it and speaks with an accent. We talked to him the other day when we were here for the open house. We stopped to look at the grotto and he told us we couldn't go in—that it was private."

"I'd like to talk to him."

They went down through the gardens and across the lawn toward the grove of trees. As they approached it, the strange man in the white robe came out and bowed to them.

"Salaam," he said.

"Good morning," said Wyatt. "Do you speak English?"

"A few words."

"I'm a policeman. My name is Wyatt. May I ask your name?"

"Ibrahim. Brother Ibrahim."

"You're Egyptian?"

"Egypt?" He smiled and shrugged. "I many things, but . . . Yes, came from Egypt here. With the marquise."

"Do you know what happened last night?"

"Happened?"

"Some jewelry belonging to Mrs. Van Gelder, the

friend of the marchioness—or the marquise as you call her—was stolen."

"Oh? Not know that. Know something bad happen, but not that."

"What do you mean, you knew something bad had happened?"

"I know. Came to me in sleep, evil god, Seth. He make snake noise." And he hissed.

"Then you didn't hear or see anything? A stranger, for instance, who might have come up through the grounds?"

"No. At night I far away—not hear, not see nothing."

Wyatt studied him, then looked past him at the entrance to the grotto, which could be dimly seen through the trees.

"Do you mind if we look in there?" he asked.

Brother Ibrahim hesitated, then shrugged.

"Is sacred place now, Temple of Ageless Wisdom, but we must all obey law—your law, my law." He bowed, touching his forehead, then gestured. "Please."

He led the way through the trees and Wyatt, Sara and Andrew followed. When they reached the grotto Andrew saw that, as he had suspected, it was completely artificial. The entrance was built of carefully selected rocks that had been cemented together and shaped so that they looked weathered and ancient. Ferns grew in recesses in the stones, most of which were covered with moss. A short distance back was a heavy wooden door with black iron hinges. Brother Ibrahim opened the door, then stepped back and let them go in. Three steps down was a long, low room that had a dark stone floor and white plastered walls. At the far end of the room was a raised platform with a square altar at its center. Two candles burned on the altar and between them, high on the rear wall, was painted a huge eye. There were wooden benches on both sides of a central aisle, and the air was heavy with the smell of incense. Bare though the room was, there was something frightening about it. Andrew wasn't sure why at first. Then he decided that it was because of the unwinking eye that watched them by the uncertain light of the candles and seemed to see everything.

"The Eye of Horus," said Wyatt, looking at the rear wall.

"Yes. Horus my master," said Ibrahim. "His sign is on me."

He opened the top of his robe and there, tattooed on his chest, was the same single, open eye and under it a bird with a savage curved beak and outstretched wings. "His eye and Horus himself as falcon."

"You celebrate mysteries here?" asked Wyatt.

Ibrahim looked at him sharply. "You are learned," he said. "Yes. We celebrate mysteries."

Wyatt nodded, and with Sara and Andrew close behind him, he walked down the central aisle to the altar. There was a door to the left of the platform. Wyatt opened it and they looked in. The room beyond was small, and the smell of incense was even stronger here, probably coming from the wooden chests and earthenware jars on the floor. Above the jars, on wooden pegs set in the wall, were some robes and a strange, looped object with a handle. The looped part was strung with wire on which there were metal discs.

"What's that?" asked Sara.

"A sistrum," said Wyatt. "You shake it like a rattle."

He opened the chests, looked into the jars, then rejoined Sara and Andrew on the platform. Brother Ibrahim had not moved; he waited patiently just inside the door. Wyatt looked around again, then went back down the aisle.

"Thank you," he said.

Brother Ibrahim bowed, let them precede him out the door, then closed it after them. Wyatt looked at the cottage just outside the grove.

"Is that where you live?" he asked.

"For now, yes. You wish there to look too?"

"If you don't mind."

"Please," he said again, and again he led the way, this time to the cottage. As before, he opened the door and let them precede him inside. The front room was simply and sparsely furnished with some chairs, a table and a chest. The kitchen, in the rear, was just as simple and ordinary; there were only two pots hanging above the stove and not much food on the shelves.

"You look for something special?" asked Ibrahim with a slight smile. "The jewels, perhaps?"

"Not necessarily," said Wyatt.

"There is other room. Here," he said and he opened a door opposite the fireplace. Wyatt looked in and his eyebrows went up slightly. Glancing past him, Andrew could see why. The room, which should have been the bedroom, was empty except for an open black coffin set on low trestles.

"Coo!" said Sara. "What's that for?"

"That where I sleep," said Ibrahim. Going over, he stepped into it and sat down with his legs crossed and arms folded.

"By why?" asked Sara.

Ibrahim shrugged. "To make remember. Have not you such a make remember in one of your prayers?" he asked Wyatt.

" 'In the midst of life we are in death,' " said Wyatt.

"Yes," said Ibrahim. He stepped out of the coffin, gestured toward it. "You would like to try?" he asked politely. "One rests there most comfortably."

"No, thank you," said Andrew, and Wyatt shook his head. He looked around the room once more, then said, "I think that's all. I'm sorry if we troubled you."

"No trouble," said Ibrahim. "A delight to have been

of service." He accompanied them to the cottage door and opened it. "May Horus watch over you and the peace of Isis be with you."

"Thank you," said Wyatt. He walked away from the cottage with Sara on one side of him and Andrew on the other. "*Quel type*, as the French would say."

"Yes," said Andrew. He had thought that Brother Ibrahim was rather odd the other day, and he was more convinced of it than ever now.

"Gave me the creeps, it did," said Sara.

"He, the temple or the coffin?" asked Andrew.

"All of them, but mostly that temple with the starey eye. Is it very old?" she asked Wyatt.

"I don't think so. The entrance was probably late eighteenth century. Landscape gardeners used to go in for follies and decorative grottoes about them. The rest of it, the temple proper, is probably quite recent. When did Brother Ibrahim come here, do you know?"

"Since Miss Tillett bought her place," said Sara. "About six months ago."

"I'd say the rest of it, the inside, was done about then."

They were almost at the gate now, and Wyatt paused and looked back at the house.

"Do you think that whoever stole the Denham diamonds stole Mrs. Van Gelder's jewels too?" asked Andrew.

"It would be very odd if it wasn't the same person or persons—an almost unbelievable coincidence. On the other hand, I couldn't find any signs of entry from the outside here, so the methods of robbery were apparently quite different."

"You've no idea who could have done it then, how or what happened to the jewels?"

"Not really, no."

"What do you do next?" asked Andrew.

"Tomorrow's my day off. I think I'll go see someone who might have some ideas about all those things."

"Who's that?" asked Andrew.

"The Baron," said Wyatt. "Baron Beasley. He has a shop on Portobello Road."

"Can we go with you?" asked Sara.

Wyatt looked down at her, hesitated a moment, then smiled.

"You're both very involved in all this, aren't you? All right. I'll pick you up at about eleven o'clock."

6

The Baron and the Wild West Show

Even Matson was impressed when Wyatt arrived the next morning. Verna was with Sara and Andrew in the front sitting room when he came in and said, "Constable Wyatt is here, madam."

"Show him in, please."

Matson stepped aside, holding the door open, and Wyatt came in. He was wearing a fawn-colored suit, clearly Saville Row, and carrying a straw boater with a club band. He looked like a typical well-dressed man about town, much younger and slimmer than he did in uniform. In fact, Andrew found it difficult to remember what he looked like when he was in uniform.

"Good morning, Miss Tillett," he said, bowing.

"Good morning, Constable. Or shouldn't I call you that when you're in mufti?"

"It doesn't matter. I hope there's no difficulty about my appointment with Sara and Andrew."

"No. Except that I wanted to make certain you really did want to take them with you."

"I wouldn't have suggested it if I didn't."

"When I questioned them, Sara admitted that she had suggested it, asked if they couldn't go with you."

"Then let's say I thought it would be a good idea. I really would like their company—they've been very help-ful on several occasions—and I assure you that they won't be in any danger."

"I'm certain of that. And in that case, I've no objec-tion."

"I told you it would be all right, didn't I?" said An-drew as Sara sighed with relief.

"Yes," said Sara.

"I take it that there have been no new developments on the robberies," said Verna.

"I wouldn't say that," said Wyatt carefully. "How-ever, while Inspector Finch may know things that I don't, I don't believe we're any closer to a solution."

"But what you're doing today is related to the rob-beries, isn't it?"

"Yes."

"Good luck, then."

"Thank you. And thank you for letting me take Sara

and Andrew. I'll give them lunch, get them back sometime late this afternoon."

Matson opened the outside door for them. There was a hansom under the porte-cochere.

"Is that yours?" asked Sara.

"Yes. I took it here, had him wait. In you go." And he helped her in, got in himself and slid over so there was room for Andrew.

"Where to now, guv'ner?" asked the cabby, opening the small trapdoor over their heads.

"Pembridge and Portobello Roads."

"Right you are."

"I love hansoms," said Sara as they went off down the driveway, rocking and swaying a little on the two rubber-tired wheels. "I think I like them even better than the landau."

"Don't let Fred hear you say that," said Andrew. Then to Wyatt, "What's the new development in the case?"

"What makes you think there is one?"

"You didn't say there wasn't when mother asked you about it. You just didn't tell her what it was."

"That's right. Well, there was still another robbery. I heard about it just before I went off duty yesterday."

"You mean a fourth one?"

"Yes. This was in Mayfair too, like Lady Damien's. A Mrs. Hartley-Seymour on Grosevenor Square."

"Jewelry?"

"Yes."

"Any clues?"

"I don't think so. The last two weren't in my district, and the only reason I know about them is that Finch came back here to get my report on the Van Gelder robbery and I heard him talking to the sergeant. He was in a real stew about it."

"I'm not surprised. Four of them in three days."

"*And* one of them a friend of the commissioner." He turned to Sara who was looking at him gravely. "Is anything the matter?"

"No. I was just wondering about something."

"What's that?"

"It's true I did ask if we could come with you today, but I wondered why you said yes."

"I told Andrew's mother why."

"And meant it?"

"Of course. It *is* a help to talk to someone about a case. And the way things are, I don't have anyone else. I mean, I can't talk to Finch. Or rather, he won't talk to me."

"Not that that would do much good."

"No. I'm afraid we don't think alike about anything."

"I should hope not," said Andrew. "Can I ask you something, sir?"

"If you drop the 'sir.' My friends call me Peter. Or did when I had friends."

That was something Andrew had wondered about. He had seen how Wyatt's family had felt about his becoming a policeman, and he wondered how the constable's friends had taken it. Now he knew.

"Who is this Baron Beasley we're going to see? You said he had a shop on Portobello Road."

"Well, he's not a fence, though I'm sure he sometimes buys and sells things that he knows have been stolen. And he's not a nose or informer, because he doesn't like the police and won't even talk to them. But I did him a good turn once, and he has occasionally been very helpful."

They went south and west, the cabby cutting skillfully in front of green Atlas buses and red ones bound for Westbourne Grove. He avoided the heavy traffic around Paddington by going over to the Bayswater Road and along that to Notting Hill Gate. Then, turning into Pembridge Road, he pulled up with a flourish.

"Here we are, sir."

Wyatt picked up a square package wrapped in brown paper that had been on the floor of the hansom, got out and helped Sara out. He paid the cabby and must have tipped him well, for the cabby saluted him extravagantly with his whip and drove off whistling.

Portobello Road was narrow, noisy and crowded. Handcarts piled high with knickknacks, bric-a-brac and gewgaws lined the street, and there were open stands in front of the shops containing books, prints, paintings, china, silver, bronzes, clothes and almost anything else you could name. They walked up the street, past men and women shouting their wares, to a small shop that had the usual oddments in front of it. In the window was a brass samovar, some glass paperweights and a marble head of Napoleon. They went in, and sitting behind the counter was the largest man Andrew had ever seen. He wasn't fat, he was huge, with a pink, smooth face, baby blue eyes and a small mouth. He wore a bottle green velvet jacket, a striped shirt and a large kingsman or brightly colored bandanna.

He grunted, looking coldly at Wyatt.

"So you've got a problem, eh?" he said, in a surprisingly thin voice and with only a slight Cockney accent.

"Have I?"

"Of course. You never come to see me any other time." He looked at Sara and Andrew. "Who are your friends?"

Wyatt introduced them, and he shook hands gravely with each of them.

"Delighted to meet you. Can't say I think much of your taste in companions, but then you're still young and you'll learn. Do you like pistachio nuts?"

"I don't think I ever had any," said Andrew.

"No? Deprived, that's what you've been. Here," and he held out a paper bag. Andrew and Sara each took some of the nuts. The shells were partly open, split apart easily, and the pistachios themselves were delicious. Beasley ate a few himself, then said to Sara, "Why are you staring at me that way? Didn't you ever see a fat man before?"

"I don't think you're fat," said Sara. "Just big. But I was wondering, are you really a baron?"

"*A* baron? I'm not a baron. I'm *the* baron. Baron Beasley of Portobello Road."

"It's not a title," said Wyatt. "Though he'd like you to think it is. It's his name. He was christened Baron."

"It's both a name *and* a title," said Beasley. "Otherwise why do they call me—" He broke off, looking at the brown paper package that Wyatt had put on the counter. "What's that?"

"What would you like it to be?" asked Wyatt.

"You know. Can I open it?"

"Go ahead. It's for you."

Beasley tore off the brown paper. Inside was a large tin labelled Pure Vermont Maple Syrup. Beasley looked at it, then sat back with a happy sigh.

"What's maple syrup?" asked Sara.

"I said that Andrew had been deprived, but apparently you've been, too. It's American, made from the sap of the sugar maple tree, and the best kind comes from Vermont."

"But what do you do with it?" asked Sara.

"Why, you eat it. You use it the way you would treacle in puddings and such, but treacle isn't in it with maple syrup. Wait." He took out a large clasp knife, punched two holes in the top of the tin and poured some of the contents into a saucer. He dipped a finger into the golden liquid and licked it off, rolling his eyes rapturously. "Here," he said to Sara and Andrew. "You try it."

They each dipped a finger in the syrup and licked it off. It *was* good, not as thick as treacle and not as cloyingly sweet.

"All right," said Beasley. "The answer is no."

"The answer to what?" asked Wyatt.

"You came here to find out if I knew anything about the Denham sparklers, right?" And when Wyatt nodded, "I told you, the answer's no."

"You're sure?"

Beasley scowled at him. "Would I say so if I wasn't?" Then, looking out of the window, "Wait a bit. Lamps!" he called.

A thin man in a ragged coat and wearing very thick spectacles was passing by. He paused and came in.

"Wotcher, Baron," he said in a hoarse voice. "How goes it?"

"Up and down like Tower Bridge," said Beasley. "Anything?"

The spectacled man hesitated, looking at Wyatt.

"You needn't worry about him," said Beasley. "He's just a copper on his day off."

The spectacled man grinned at this new example of Beasley's humor, then shook his head.

"Nothing," he said. "I was just talking to the Dutchman. He's been keeping a glim in the window late and early, but no one's been near him."

"What I thought," said Beasley. "If anything shows, you'll let me know?"

Lamps nodded and left.

"Who's the Dutchman?" asked Wyatt.

"The biggest jewelry fence in London, specializes in diamonds. He'd take in the Kohinoor without turning a hair. Yes, and get rid of it overnight."

"What about a string of Cartier pearls?"

"No sign of them either."

"What do you think it means, Baron?"

Beasley shrugged. "Dunno. None of the regulars were in on them. They wish they were because they were a set of rorty jobs, but none of them had anything to do with them. They're saying it's a new gang, maybe foreign, that they're holding the stuff, not going to pass it and they don't like it."

"Then they'll keep their eyes open, too?"

"Sure to. If I hear anything, I'll let you know. You're still at the section-house?"

"Yes. Wellington Road. Come on, you two."

Wyatt was frowning as they left, started down the street towards Pembridge Road.

"I'm not sure I understood him," said Andrew. "Just what did he mean?"

"That none of the best known of the London burglars were involved in the thefts. Since that's so, they think perhaps a foreign gang is responsible and of course they don't like it. So if any of them hears anything, comes across any kind of a clue, they'll let the Baron know."

"Does that happen often, criminals helping the police?"

"Much more often than the public realizes. A great deal of police information comes from informers." He glanced at Sara. "Is something puzzling you too?"

"Yes. Where did you get that maple syrup?"

"From an American sea captain I met when I first joined the force and walked a beat near the docks. Why?"

"I just wondered. I don't think I ever met an American."

"Well, I don't know whether you'll have a chance to meet one, but you'll see quite a few after we have lunch."

"Why?" asked Sara. "Where are we going?"

"To the Olympia."

"What's at the Olympia?" asked Andrew.

"I know," said Sara, her eyes large. "At least, I think I do. Isn't it Buffalo Bill's Wild West Show?"

"It is."

"Coo! Lumme! I'd rather see that than anything in London! Except Miss Tillett's play," she added hastily. "But why are you taking us there? It doesn't have anything to do with the robberies, does it?"

"No, but you know what they say about all work and no play. And the truth is that I've been anxious to see the show ever since it came here, but it's no fun going alone."

He smiled as he said it but, in spite of his light tone, Andrew suspected that he was telling the truth—that he hadn't wanted to go alone—which gave Andrew a clearer picture than ever of Wyatt's isolation and loneliness.

They took a four-wheeler to Kensington High Street, had lunch at a café and then crossed over to the Olympia. Andrew had never been there before, and, though he knew it was large—there had been ten thousand people there for a recent military show—he was surprised at its size. Wyatt had a bit of a discussion with the man at the ticket office and he must have been very specific for when they were shown to their seats they proved to be in the front row in the middle of the auditorium, so close to the performers that at times they could have reached out and touched them.

They had barely taken their seats when the band struck up a stirring march, the big double doors at the end of the auditorium swung open and Buffalo Bill—Colonel Cody—rode out into the amphitheatre. He looked exactly like his pictures on the posters outside the Olympia. He was very distinguished looking, with grey hair that hung down to his shoulders and a short, pointed beard and mustache. He wore a fringed buckskin jacket and leggings and a wide-brimmed felt hat, which he took off in response to the applause that greeted him. He was riding a magnificent chestnut horse, and when he bowed, the horse bowed too and to continued applause they made a circuit of the ring, the horse rearing, prancing and dancing.

There was considerable discussion later on as to what they liked best in the show. Wyatt's choice was Annie Oakley, who was even more elegant than Buffalo Bill in her costume of white deerskin. Though she looked like a young girl, with her braids hanging down her back, she handled her rifle as no marksman in any army in the world could have done, breaking glass balls tossed in the air right and left and behind her, even when three were tossed up at once, and she ended her act by shooting the pips out of a playing card some fifty feet behind her back, shooting over her shoulder and using a mirror to sight with.

Much as Andrew admired Annie Oakley, what impressed him most was the riding: the whooping cowboys, who were able to stay in the saddle during the bucking bronco contests, when the horse was not only twisting and turning but bouncing up in the air with all four feet off the ground.

Sara's favorites were the spectacles—of which there were several; a buffalo hunt, an Indian attack on Pony Express riders, and an attack on a covered wagon train. It was before the last of these, the act that closed the show, that Andrew saw something of no real importance but which intrigued him as much as the elaborate spectacles.

A cowboy had given an exhibition of roping: lassoing a steer, then a galloping horseman and finally three horsemen together. He was directly in front of them when he finished his turn, and as the arena was being cleared, he took out a small bag and a square of paper and shook some of the contents of the bag into the paper.

"What's he doing?" asked Andrew.

"Making a cigarette," said Wyatt. "It's called rolling your own. Watch." Licking one side of the paper so that it would stick, the cowboy rolled it deftly into a tube and lit it by flicking his thumbnail across the head of a match.

"How do you know so much about it?" asked Andrew.

"I spent well over a year in America before I joined the police, about half that time in the West. That was something else that Holmes liked to talk to me about because he spent quite a lot of time in America too."

The arena had been cleared. A covered wagon, drawn by a pair of horses, came out of the double doors, followed by a second and a third. As they began a slow circuit of the amphitheatre, there were a series of shrill whoops and a war party of Indians came galloping out after them. Cracking their whips, the drivers swung the covered wagons around so that they formed a circle in the center of the arena. Using this as a barricade, they, the other men and women too, began firing at the Indians who were now circling the wagons at a full gallop, shooting over their horse's heads and sometimes under their necks and even under their bellies. Andrew had never seen such horsemanship, for the Indians were riding bareback and without stirrups. Then, when the battle was at its peak, the circle of attacking Indians drawing closer and closer, there was a bugle call and out swept the cavalry, led by Buffalo Bill. There was a sharp exchange of gunfire in which many of the Indians fell, then the rest fled.

Sara sat silent and serious during the cheers and applause that followed.

"Does it always end like that?" she asked.

"I imagine so," said Wyatt. "Why?"

"I don't think it's right," she said. "I think the Indians should win sometimes."

Andrew and Wyatt exchanged glances.

"I'm inclined to agree with you," said Wyatt.

The crowd that was leaving the Olympia was so large that it took them some time to get a hansom, and it was well after five when they got back to St. John's Wood. Andrew asked Wyatt if he wouldn't like to come in for tea, but he said it was late and he should be getting along.

"Where?" asked Andrew. "We don't know where you live."

"At the moment I'm in the section-house next to the Wellington Road Police Station."

"What's a section-house?" asked Sara.

"A kind of dormitory for unmarried policemen. I have

a cubicle, bed and locker there." He caught the look on Andrew's face. "It's not bad. It's something like army barracks."

Andrew nodded. "When will we see you again?" he asked.

"Unless Finch needs me for something, I'll be walking my beat around here again tomorrow. But if I hear anything from Beasley, I'll let you know."

"It was a wonderful day," said Sara seriously. "I don't think we'll ever forget it. Thank you very much."

"No," said Wyatt, just as seriously. "Thank *you*."

He waved to them, got into the hansom, and it moved off.

7

The Vanishing Corpse

One consequence of the afternoon at the Olympia was a quarrel between Andrew and Fred. After telling Verna about the show, naturally he wanted to go riding the next morning, and she agreed that she would go, too. When Fred came back from Three Oaks with the horse he had borrowed for Andrew, he found Andrew riding Verna's hunter bareback around the yard and flew into a rage, saying that the place for naked savages who rode that way was America and not St. John's Wood and that he had no intention of working for one. When Andrew tried to point out the lack of logic in this statement, Fred became angrier than ever, and it took Verna's arrival and all her diplomacy to calm him down.

While they were riding, Andrew asked Verna when he and Sara were going to see her play, and she said that, if they wanted to, they could come that night. So that evening, after a certain amount of hectic female preparation—for Mrs. Wiggins had been invited to go with Sara and Andrew—Fred drove them to the theatre where Mr. Harrison, the manager, escorted them to one of the boxes.

Until that moment Andrew had found it difficult to understand Verna's reluctance to let him see her perform. After all, if the critics liked her, what difference did it make what he thought? But at the theatre he was suddenly seized with anxiety. Suppose he had some reservations about her performance, found it awkward, shallow or false, what then? Should he say so, or lie about it? It was no easy decision to make because Verna was very sensitive and acute, and if he did lie she would undoubtedly know it and that would make things even worse.

He need not have worried. A few minutes after the curtain rose on the sunny parlor of the squire's country house, Verna came in with an armful of flowers she had supposedly cut in the garden; and by the time she had put them in vases, she had completely captivated Andrew as she had the critics and everyone else. Later, looking back at the play, he realized how contrived it was; the story of a young woman who discovers that she is not only adopted but illegitimate and must decide whether to reject the mother who has just found her or to jeopardize her relationship with the young marquis who wants to marry her. But because of Verna's artistry, he was completely unaware of the play's shortcomings at the time and, while not weeping like Sara, Mrs. Wiggins and most of the women in the audience, at the final curtain he was so affected that it was several minutes before he was able to join the tumultuous applause.

Harrison took them backstage to Verna's dressing room afterward and, uncertain as to just how he could tell her how he felt about her acting, Andrew found he did not have to say anything. For, taking one swift look at his face, she flushed with pleasure and became very busy trying to put Sara and Mrs. Wiggins at their ease.

They had decided earlier to have dinner at Bentley's, one of Andrew's favorite restaurants, and by the time Verna had changed and Fred had driven them there, Sara and her mother had both recovered and begun to behave normally.

They were shown to a corner table, ordered oysters, and were just finishing them when a tall, fair man and an older, grey-haired man with a military mustache came in. They were both in evening clothes, and as the head waiter was seating them with a good deal of deference, the fair man saw Verna, said something to his companion, and they both came towards her.

"Good evening, Miss Tillett," he said, bowing. "I don't know if you remember me, but we met at Mr. Sherlock Holmes's."

"Of course I remember. It's Lord Lowther, isn't it?"

"It is. In different ways and to different degrees we were both involved in the same case."

"We were indeed," said Verna smiling. "I believe you know Sara Wiggins, better known as Screamer, and my son, Andrew. And this is Mrs. Wiggins, Sara's mother."

"I certainly do know Sara and Andrew. They helped save my life. As for Mrs. Wiggins, I met her when I tried to show my appreciation for what Sara had done for me."

"You didn't just try," said Mrs. Wiggins. "You were very generous—more than generous."

"I don't agree," said Lord Lowther, "but we won't discuss that now." Then, turning back to Verna, "May I present an admirer of yours, Mr. Howard Wendell of Scotland Yard?"

"I'm always happy to meet an admirer," said Verna, extending her hand to the grey-haired man. "Though I don't know on what you base your admiration."

"On several things," said Wendell. "But mostly on your acting. We were at the theatre tonight, and when we saw you here, I asked Lord Lowther, who said he had met you, if he would introduce me so I could tell you that I thought your performance was one of the finest I've ever seen."

"You're very kind," said Verna. "It's probably just as well that I didn't know that you were in the audience. I had difficulty enough coping with the thought that Andrew, who had never seen me on the stage before, was there."

"Oh?" said Wendell, turning to Andrew. "And were you as impressed as I was?"

"Yes, sir," said Andrew. "Did Lord Lowther say you were at Scotland Yard?"

"Mr. Wendell is a divisional superintendent," said Lowther. "One of the so-called Big Four."

"I never did understand the reason for the adjective," said Wendell. "We don't call the commissioner 'the Big *One.*' But . . . Yes, I am at Scotland Yard. And another of the things I have admired you for, Miss Tillett, is the way you've been conducting yourself with the press and in general following the theft of the Denham diamonds."

"I don't feel I did anything unusual," said Verna. "I just told the press that I had every confidence in the police. That I was certain that they would get to the bottom of the crimes."

"Well, that was a very helpful statement. Not like some that have been made lately, which were very critical of us . . ."

"Have there been any new developments in any of the cases?" asked Verna in carefully neutral tones.

"Well, no," said Wendell somewhat awkwardly. "But I'm sure there will be. Inspector Finch, who is heading the investigation, is one of our best men."

"He is?" said Verna with just the faintest shadow of surprise.

"Oh. I thought I heard something, then I heard your door. Who is it?"

"I don't know. I couldn't tell that or what he was doing, but I thought I'd go outside and see."

"I'll come with you."

They went down the stairs, keeping close to the wall so that the treads would not creak. It took a little time to open the door since it was not only locked and bolted, but chained. They left it ajar, crossed the driveway and ran down alongside it, staying on the grass because it was quieter. When they reached the hedge that separated the garden from the street, Andrew held up his hand. They crouched down, spread the leaves of the hedge and looked through. The man was still there and now, with the street light behind him, they could see him more clearly. He was a big man, wearing a billycock hat, and he was looking at the wall of Three Oaks and tapping one foot impatiently.

"Can you tell who he is?" asked Sara in a whisper.

Andrew shook his head. He was fairly sure he didn't know the man, hadn't seen him before, but he couldn't be certain because with the light behind him, he could not make out his features.

"Let's go round," whispered Sara, pointing to the street. "Then we can see."

Andrew hesitated. If they went out to the street, they would be able to see the man more clearly, but, by the same token, if the man turned around, he would be able to see them.

"I'm not sure . . ." he began, but by that time Sara was gone. Frowning, he bent down, looked through the hedge again. The man was still there, still looking at the wall. As Andrew straightened up, out of the corner of his eye he saw something—a shadow—coming across Rysdale Road behind the man. He hurried after Sara and caught her at the edge of the driveway.

"Wait," he whispered. "Be careful."

"I know. We don't want him to see us."

"It's not just that. I thought I saw someone—"

He broke off as they heard a curious noise that sounded like a sigh, followed by a thud. They looked at one another, then peered around the end of the hedge. The man was no longer standing. He was lying face down on the pavement, his head just a short distance from the wall.

Andrew gripped Sara's shoulder, holding her there. They looked up the street, to the right and to the left. There was no sign of any movement, no sound.

Sara put her mouth close to his ear. "What happened to him?" she whispered.

"I don't know. We'd better see."

Slowly they went up the street, paused when they reached the man. His face was turned slightly sideways, and they could see one eye. It was open, staring. He was, as Andrew had thought, powerfully built. His hair grew low on his forehead, the visible ear was battered, misshapen, and what they could see of his face was brutal.

"Is he dead?" asked Sara, her voice unnaturally loud and clear.

Andrew knew he must be. That open eye was not merely staring and unblinking, something was gone from it. Besides, no one could lie that still if he were not dead. However . . . He bent down and looked more closely at the man. He was rather flashily dressed in a checked jacket, and there was a dark stain between his shoulder blades. Andrew touched it, then drew back and stood up. It was blood. Feeling a little sick, he thrust his hand into the pocket of his robe, wiping his fingers again and again.

"Yes," he said. "He's dead."

"What are we going to do?"

"We'd better get the police."

"We can wake Fred, send him to the police station the way your mother did after the robbery."

He nodded. Then as they started back towards the house, "Wait a minute. There must be a policeman around here somewhere."

"Where?"

"I don't know, but there must be. And if we can find one, we can save a lot of time. Why don't you go that way and I'll go this. If either of us finds a policeman we'll bring him back here. If we don't find one, we'll wake Fred."

"All right," said Sara. Turning, her hair flying, she ran up Rysdale Road past their house. Circling wide around the still body, Andrew ran the other way, along the wall that surrounded Three Oaks. He still felt a little sick, and he suddenly realized that he had continued to wipe his hand on his robe. Did he just feel sick or was he frightened too? Of course he was frightened. It was one thing to play being a detective with Peter Wyatt, look for clues, speculate on how the several different robberies had been committed and by whom. But what had just happened had changed things completely, for whoever had killed the man in the checked jacket would not hesitate to kill again. And now Andrew knew, not just how suddenly death could come, but how final it was.

He glanced through the closed gates of Three Oaks as he ran by. There was no sign of a light in the big house. There were no lights in any of the widely separated houses on the other side of the road. He reached the corner, looked right and left, saw no policeman, and turned left so as to complete the circuit and end up back at their house again. He was still running when he came to the next corner, but not quite so fast for he was beginning to get a stitch in his side and his feet were starting to hurt. The thin soles of his slippers were not made for running on pavement. This time he stopped when he looked right and left. Had they been foolish to think that there would be a policeman walking his beat somewhere in the area at night? Perhaps. He went on at a trot, through the occasional yellow pools cast by the gaslights, but mostly through the darkness. That street ahead of him was Rysdale Road. When he reached it, he would walk the rest of the way and . . .

With sudden anxiety he wondered what had happened to Sara. Going in opposite directions around the same area, they should have met before this. In spite of the pain in his side, he began to run again. Reaching Rysdale Road, he looked right as he started to go around the corner—and there she was! Not only that, but there was a policeman with her.

Andrew stopped, waiting for them, and the intensity of his relief was the measure of how anxious he had been. That was why they had not met. When Sarah reached the corner she must have looked up Rysdale Road, seen the constable and, instead of making the circuit around Three Oaks as Andrew had done, had gone straight on.

They came towards him, the policeman, tall and helmeted, not appearing to hurry but forcing Sara to trot to keep up with him.

"Now then," said the officer, looking down at Andrew, "Who's this?"

"The boy I told you about," said Sara. "Andrew Tillett."

"Ho yus," said the constable. "And where's this body you found?"

"There," said Sara.

"Where?"

"There," said Andrew, turning and pointing. He could have found the place with his eyes closed; about fifteen feet from where their hedge ended and the wall of Three Oaks made a right angle. He stiffened, leaned forward a little as Sara was doing. The pavement was empty. There was no sign of a body.

8

Finch's Fury

"You're sure this is where he was standing?" asked Finch.

Andrew looked at Sara. "Yes," he said.

"How do you know?"

"I just do. I told you, I saw him first from my room—"

"*Thought* you saw him, saw someone."

"All right—thought I saw someone. It couldn't have been much further up the street because the wall of Three Oaks would have cut off my view. Then when Sara and I came downstairs—"

"Just a second. Did she see him, too—this man—from upstairs in your house?"

"No. Something woke her. When she heard my door open, she came out into the hall. And when I told her what I'd seen, she said we should go down and see who it was. So we did."

It was a little after nine the next morning, and they were gathered there on Rysdale Road; Sara, Andrew, Inspector Finch, Peter Wyatt and Verna. Verna had awakened when the constable walked Sara and Andrew back to the house. He had been obviously incredulous and rather annoyed, and it's doubtful whether he would even have reported the occurrence if Verna, after a quick glance at Sara and Andrew, had not insisted on it. As a result, Finch, accompanied by Wyatt, had appeared at the house at a little before nine, and when he questioned the young people Verna, though she kept to the background, stayed with them.

"What time did you say this was?"

"Three thirty."

"What time did you get to bed?"

"About twelve thirty."

"Do you usually go to bed that late?"

"No. But I told you we'd been to theatre first and to Bentley's afterward for a late supper."

It was clear to Andrew that these questions of Finch's were not casual—that they were leading somewhere—but he was not sure where.

"Ah, yes. And exactly what did you eat?"

Wyatt, standing behind Finch and taking notes, looked at Finch and then at Andrew. Andrew had a feeling that he was trying to tell him something, but he wasn't sure what.

"Oysters and lobster."

Finch had looked even more harried than usual when he arrived. Now, for the first time, he relaxed a little.

"Lobster is not easy to digest," he said. "Especially at that hour."

Verna stirred. "Are you suggesting that Andrew imagined it?" she asked quietly.

"Imagined it or dreamed it. Don't you think that's possible?"

"That he and Sara both imagined or dreamed exactly the same thing? No."

"But did Sara see anything at all?" asked Finch with exaggerated and exasperating patience. "Your son wakes from a sleep that has not been very restful. Like many boys his age he reads penny dreadfuls that are full of mystery and murder—and such things are more in his thoughts now than ever because of the theft of your jewels. So he thinks he sees a man lurking in the street, thinks he sees him murdered. And Miss Sara, younger than he is and therefore easily influenced, sees whatever he thinks he sees. As a matter of fact," he concluded with obvious satisfaction, "the thing that convinced me that what they described did not happen is the fact that their stories are so exactly alike, with none of the slight differences one expects from two independent witnesses."

"If you'll forgive me, Inspector," said Wyatt with a polite cough. "There was one small difference in their stories."

Finch turned and looked at him with more surprise

than annoyance. "What was that?"

"Master Andrew thought he saw someone come across the road. Miss Sara didn't."

"What of it?"

"Possibly nothing, sir. But I thought . . . There's a large tree there. If someone was waiting here—near the wall—and someone else was hiding there behind the tree . . ."

"If!" said Finch, his face suddenly flushed. "What are you suggesting? That someone slipped across the street, killed the mysterious lurker and then disappeared into thin air, taking the body with him?"

"No, sir," said Wyatt. "It couldn't have happened that way because the body didn't disappear right away."

"It couldn't have happened that way because there *was* no body!" Suddenly aware of Verna's gaze, he checked himself. "I'm sorry, ma'am," he said. "I suppose I shouldn't lose my patience and my temper, but I've been under a great deal of pressure from the press, the insurance companies *and* the commissioner. After all, we've had a disappearance and five major robberies during the past few days. And while I'm not convinced there's any connection between them, there are some who think there is. As for the young people's story, I'm not saying that they don't believe what they've told us. And if there'd been any evidence at all to back it up, any signs of a struggle or any blood here on the pavement . . ."

Andrew stiffened. "Could you come back to the house for a moment, Inspector?" he asked.

"What? What for?"

"I just remembered something—something I'd like to show you."

Finch looked at Andrew, then at Verna. This was his opportunity to make amends for his burst of temper.

"Of course," he said. And stepping back politely, he let Verna precede him up the street. Sara and Andrew fell in behind him, one on each side of Wyatt.

"What are you going to show him?" asked Sara quietly.

"You'll see," said Andrew.

Wyatt, walking between them, had closed his notebook and was looking straight ahead of him. Andrew felt a tap on his wrist and, looking down, saw that Wyatt was holding out a folded piece of paper. He took it—it was a page from Wyatt's notebook—unfolded it and read: "As soon as possible, search around tree across street for clues. P.W."

Andrew looked up at him, but Wyatt was still looking straight ahead with no particular expression on his face. Andrew hesitated. He wouldn't be able to do what Wyatt wanted for some time. Reaching around behind Wyatt, he tapped Sara's arm as Wyatt had tapped his, passed her the note. She frowned as she read it, glanced at Wyatt, at Andrew and nodded. She stepped aside and bent down apparently to fasten a button on one of her shoes. As Andrew turned in at the driveway, he looked back and saw her hurrying across the street to the tree.

Matson opened the front door for them. Finch followed Verna in, then said, "All right, young man. What did you want to show me?"

"I'll get it," said Andrew.

He ran up the stairs to his room. He had never really examined it, and if he was wrong he was going to look like an awful fool. He went into his room, picked up his bathrobe and glanced inside the right-hand pocket. Then he ran down the stairs again. Verna and Wyatt looked at him with interest, Finch with a patronizing smile.

"I only remembered this when you said you might believe us if there'd been any blood or signs of a struggle," said Andrew. "I told you there was blood on the back of the body. What I didn't tell you was that I touched it, got some of the blood on my fingers and wiped it off on the inside of my pocket."

He pulled out the pocket, turning it inside out, and there were several distinct darkish streaks.

"Well, Inspector?" said Verna.

Finch took the bathrobe from Andrew, studied the stains, felt them and then said, "Let me see your hand, your right hand."

Andrew held it out. "If you're looking for traces of blood there," he said, "I not only wiped it on the bathrobe, I've washed my hands since then."

"I don't think that's what Inspector Finch was looking

for, darling," said Verna in a neutral voice. "I think he wanted to see if you'd cut your hand somehow, got blood in the pocket that way."

Finch shot a quick glance at her. "I didn't think he'd done that. I just wanted to rule it out. Because I'm sure you'll admit that even if what he told us is true, there's still something very odd about it. According to their story, they were only gone a few minutes. The girl, Sara, went east until she met Constable Dignam, but she didn't leave Rysdale Road and neither she nor the constable saw any kind of vehicle go up or down the street. Well, if that's true, what happened to the body? Who took it away, where and how?"

Andrew knew that this was the weak spot in their story, and he had no answer to it. He glanced at Finch, then at Wyatt. Catching his eye, Wyatt looked down, then up to a point well above Andrew's head. Andrew stared at him. Again he knew Wyatt was trying to tell him something, but he wasn't sure what. Then it came to him.

"The wall!" he said. "The wall around Three Oaks!"

"What about it?" asked Finch.

"I think what Master Andrew was wondering," said Wyatt, "was whether it wasn't possible that the body was put over the wall."

"Put over it how?"

"Perhaps pulled over it with a rope."

"Are you saying," said Finch to Andrew, "that there

was not only a murder, but that the murderer had an accomplice at Three Oaks?"

"I've no idea," said Andrew. "I just thought that maybe that's what had happened to the body."

Finch looked at him as if he wished he didn't exist.

"The marchioness isn't going to like it," he said. "She's annoyed enough already because we haven't recovered Mrs. Van Gelder's jewels. And I don't expect to find anything, but I suppose I'd better go over there and look."

"I certainly think you should," said Verna. "And I think you and Sara should go too, Andrew. You not only know where the body was—you also know the grounds at Three Oaks." And without giving Finch a chance to object, she told Matson to have Fred bring the carriage around as quickly as possible. It was only then that she said, "Where *is* Sara?"

"She'll be along in a minute," said Andrew evasively.

And she was. Though it only took Fred a few minutes to bring the landau around to the porte-cochere, when they went out Sara was coming up the driveway.

"We're going over to Three Oaks," said Andrew, and he told her why. She nodded, and she and Andrew got into the carriage.

"Are you coming too, ma'am?" Finch asked Verna.

"I don't think you need me," she said.

"Probably not," he said. And bowing to her, he and Wyatt got into the landau, too. Fred shook the reins, and the horses trotted off. Finch, frowning, was grim and silent until the carriage drew up in front of the door at Three Oaks.

"Stay here," he said to Wyatt, getting out and ignoring Sara and Andrew. "I'll tell the marchioness we're here and what we want to do."

Wyatt saluted. He, Sara and Andrew got out also, and when Finch had disappeared inside, he said to Sara, "That was a difficult assignment I gave you. I didn't even have a chance to tell you what to look for."

"Did you know what you wanted me to look for?"

"Not really," he said with a smile. "Did you find anything?"

"This," she said, taking something out of her pocket and giving it to him. "If it is anything."

In some ways it looked like a cigarette butt and in some ways it didn't. For while it consisted of tobacco and paper, the tobacco was very fine and loose, not packed tightly as most cigarettes are. And when it was stepped on—as it had apparently been—instead of becoming a flattened tube, it had opened up so that the paper was merely folded over the tobacco.

"Yes, it certainly is something," said Wyatt, studying it. "You found it near the tree?"

"Yes," said Sara. "Behind it."

"What is it?" asked Andrew.

"What does it look like?"

"A cigarette stub, but a funny one."

"Right," said Wyatt. He had been writing something in his notebook. He tore out the page, wrapped the paper and tobacco in it, and gave it to Andrew. "I don't have any safe place to keep it over at the section-house. Would you keep it for me?"

"Of course," said Andrew. He looked at the paper before he put it in his pocket, saw that Wyatt had dated it and stated where it had been found. He knew that Sherlock Holmes had been a great expert on tobacco, able to identify over a hundred different kinds by their ash alone, and he wondered if Wyatt was just as knowledgeable and what he had made of this particular clue.

Finch came out of the house, still looking bad-tempered.

"All right," he said. "The marchioness was just as irritated as I thought she'd be, but she gave me permission to go where I want, talk to anyone I want. Now it's your idea that this corpus of yours was put over the wall?" he said to Andrew.

"Yes, sir. Put over or pulled over with a rope."

"And you know where?"

"I wouldn't say that, but I think I can find the place inside here that's nearest to where we saw it outside."

"All right. Show us."

With Sara and Andrew leading the way, they went down through the terraces and the formal gardens. Still grim and busy with his own thoughts, Finch did not notice the grotto or the whitewashed cottage, or if he did, did not comment. But though the others glanced at them as they went by, they did not see any sign of Brother Ibrahim.

When they were almost at the wall, Andrew and Sara paused for a brief conference, then went on to a point some fifteen or twenty feet from the corner where the wall made a right angle and ran back from the road.

"We think it was right about here, Inspector," said Andrew.

"What? Oh, yes," said Finch, and leaving the gravel path, he started to cross the flower bed that lay between the path and the wall.

"Wait!" said Sara, shocked. "What are you doing?"

She looked at Andrew, who frowned at her, then at Wyatt who shrugged. Andrew knew why she was upset. If there were any footprints or signs that the body had been dragged through there, Finch was effectively destroying them. If Finch heard Sara, however, he gave no sign of it.

"Well?" he said, looking around. "Where did the body go from here, if it ever was here?"

Andrew didn't think that anything would be gained by pointing out that Finch had made it impossible for anyone to find or read any clues in the ground, so he said, "Don't you think there might be something on top of the wall?"

"On top of the wall?"

"Yes. I saw the head gardener in one of the greenhouses. If you asked him, I'm sure he'd get you a ladder. Or . . ." He turned to Wyatt. "If you gave me a leg up, I could take a look."

"Of course," said Wyatt. And before Finch could protest, he clasped his hands together, Andrew placed one foot in them, and Wyatt lifted him up high enough so that he could scramble to the top of the wall.

"Do you see anything?" asked Sara as he kneeled there, studying the top of the wall.

"I'm not sure," said Andrew.

"You mean there are no bloody handprints?" said Finch ironically. "No trails of blood?"

"No," said Andrew, crawling a few feet to the right, "but there are a few scrapes on top of the wall—as if something had been dragged over it—and . . . Hello!" He picked something up.

"What is it?" asked Sara.

"I'll show you when I get down." Swinging his feet over, he lowered himself as far as he could and dropped to the ground. "Look at this," he said, holding up some brownish filaments.

"It looks as if it came off a rope," said Sara.

"That's what I think," said Andrew. "That it's hemp that was rubbed off and caught in cracks in the bricks."

"And that's all you can tell us?" said Finch.

"Well, in any case it does prove that something was pulled over the wall," said Andrew patiently.

"Of course. Your famous corpse that disappeared once

from Rysdale Road and then disappeared again here." He turned as footsteps crunched on the gravel path behind him. "Who the devil's this?"

"Salaam, *effendi*," said Brother Ibrahim, bowing to Wyatt. "Salaam, my young friends."

"His name is Ibrahim, Brother Ibrahim," said Wyatt. "He came here from Egypt with the marchioness, lives in that cottage back there."

"What does he do?" asked Finch. "Sell rugs?"

"No, sir. He's a priest of the Temple of Ageless Wisdom."

"What's that? Never mind, don't tell me. And tell him to go away. He can't help us."

"I wonder," said Wyatt, slowly.

"What do you mean?"

"His cottage is quite close to the road, and I gather he's a light sleeper. Don't you think it might be useful to find out if he heard or saw anything?"

"Heard or saw what? The corpse that never was?" Turning to Brother Ibrahim, he said, "Spik English?"

"Yes, *effendi*. A little."

"Well, these two claim that a murder was committed around here last night," said Finch, raising his voice as if that would make him easier to understand. "You savvy murder?" and he drew his finger across his throat.

"I understand," said Brother Ibrahim.

"They also think that the body was pulled over the wall and may be around here somewhere."

"It's not just around," said Andrew. "If it is here anywhere—and I'm sure it is—it's been hidden or buried. Did you hear or see anything that could help us find it?" Then as the Egyptian hesitated, "The other day, when Mrs. Van Gelder's jewels were stolen, you said you knew something bad had happened because the evil god Seth came to you in your sleep and made a snake noise. Did anything like that happen last night?"

Brother Ibrahim looked at him admiringly. "The young one not only remembers, but understands. Yes. My sleep was disturbed again last night."

"Disturbed how?" asked Andrew.

Ibrahim shrugged. "I have not the words for it. But still I may be able to help you. Wait here a moment." And he walked off some fifteen or twenty feet, sank down gracefully onto the grass with his legs crossed and his back to them.

"What's he doing?" asked Finch.

"I don't know," said Andrew. "But he told us to wait here."

"He told us!" said Finch scornfully, and he marched off after the Egyptian and paused looking down at him. Sara, Andrew and Wyatt followed slowly. Ibrahim was sitting there with his eyes closed and the tips of his fingers pressed to his forehead.

"What *is* he doing?" Sara asked Andrew in a hushed voice.

"I'm not sure. Maybe meditating. Or maybe he's put himself into a trance."

"And what are we supposed to do, wait here till he comes out of it?" asked Finch. "Hey, you. Wake up!"

"Don't do that," said Sara. "He said he might be able to help us. Or"—she looked sharply at Finch—"don't you want him to help us?"

Before Finch could answer, Brother Ibrahim opened his eyes.

"Yes," he said. "There *is* something here—an Osiris. It is buried . . . there!" and he pointed to a place near one of the greenhouses.

"A what?" asked Finch.

"He means a corpse," said Wyatt. "The ancient Egyptians called everyone who died the Osiris."

"And he got that from sitting there with his eyes closed?"

"However he did it, don't you think we should go look?" said Andrew. "It should be easy enough to tell whether something's been buried there or not."

"All right," Finch said to the Egyptian. "Show me where."

Brother Ibrahim rose and walked across the lawn to a large bush some four or five feet high.

"Here," he said, pointing down.

They had all followed him and now looked down. The turf had been cut in a circle around the bush and there was no question but that the soil had been freshly turned.

"I think he's even balmier than the rest of you," said Finch. "But we'll look." He jerked his head at a spade that had been thrust into a compost pit full of grass clippings, leaves and dead flowers. "Get that," he said to Wyatt, "and start digging."

Wyatt saluted, got the spade and set to work. He had only taken a few shovelsful, making a neat pile of the loose soil he dug up, when the door of the nearest greenhouse burst open and a squat, gnomelike man wearing an ancient, wide-brimmed straw hat came hurrying out.

"What the devil are you doing?" he said angrily.

"What does it look like?" asked Finch. Then, looking him up and down. "Who are you, anyway?"

"I'm Parr, the head gardener here," he said with a broad Somerset accent. "Who are you?"

"Inspector Finch of Scotland Yard."

"I don't believe you! Since when did the police go around vandalizing people's gardens?"

"Who's vandalizing your garden?"

"What do you call what you're doing to my *Indicum-Roseum?*"

"Your what?"

"My *Indicum-Roseum!*" he repeated, pointing to the bush.

"Oh. I've been given information that a body was buried here. I doubt it myself, but I've got to make sure, so we're going to dig up your Indian rose, or whatever it is, and see."

"You'll do no such thing!" said Parr. "Give me that!" And he wrenched the spade away from Wyatt.

"I told you that I'm looking for a body," said Finch with barely controlled fury. "That means that a serious crime may have been committed—which is why the marchioness gave me permission to go where I want, do what I want. If you don't give that spade back to the constable at once, I'll arrest you for interfering with the police in the performance of their duty!"

"The mistress gave you permission to dig up the *Indicum?*"

"She did."

Parr threw down the shovel, ripped off his hat and hurled that to the ground, too.

"I'll give her my notice!" he shouted. "As daft as any in Bedlam she be! Since early April she's been at me to move it so she could see it from the breakfast room window. 'I'll not!' I told her. 'Three years I've been nursing it in the greenhouse. This is it's first spring out of doors, and I'll not move it till it's bloomed—not for the queen herself!' Well, last week it finished blooming, yesterday I transplanted it, and now she's letting you dig it up again."

"She is," said Finch. "Get on with it, Wyatt."

But as Wyatt bent down, Parr snatched the spade himself.

"No!" he said. "If it must be done, I'll do it. I'll not have a clumsy policeman injuring the roots. From the state of Virginia in America it came," he said, pushing the spade skillfully into the ground with his foot, "the only one of this kind and this color that I know of. And what it thinks of the way we're treating it, I don't know and don't want to know!"

He put the dirt on the pile Wyatt had started and continued digging in sullen silence. Working carefully, he dug down two or more feet completely around the bush, then levered it up with the spade and, with Wyatt's help, lifted it out and put it to one side.

"Well, there you are," he said. "Where's your body?"

They all looked down at the hole which was some four feet in diameter and almost three feet deep. It was clear that the earth beneath the bush had not been disturbed, but having gone this far, Finch was stubborn.

"If it's there, it's deeper than that," he said. "Keep digging."

"Not I," said Parr, throwing down the spade. "It's my opinion that the only thing that's buried there is your brains. If you want any more digging done, do it yourself." And he marched off towards the greenhouse.

"How dare you talk to me that way!" roared Finch. "Come back here!"

But the gardener ignored him, went into the greenhouse and closed the door. His face flushed with rage,

Finch glared after him, then said, "All right, Wyatt. You dig."

"Yes, Inspector," said Wyatt. Taking off his helmet and tunic, he picked up the spade and began to dig. Convinced that they were wasting time and effort for no purpose, Andrew looked sympathetically at Wyatt. But, as always, Wyatt did not seem too disturbed. Catching Andrew's eye, he glanced toward the compost pit where he had found the spade. Andrew was not certain he knew what Wyatt wanted him to do, but the sign was as unmistakable as the others had been. Moving back slowly from between Sara and Brother Ibrahim, he circled around behind Finch and drifted toward the compost pit. He saw something white on the ground a few feet from it and picked it up. It was a cigarette butt like the one Sara had found behind the tree; the tobacco rather loose and the paper open rather than pasted into a tube. He didn't know if the cigarette stub itself had any significance, but the fact that a second one had been found here did: it would indicate that whoever had waited behind the tree had also been in Three Oaks. Wyatt must have seen it when he went to get the spade, but conscious of Finch's hostility, he had not wanted to pick it up himself.

Wrapping the cigarette butt in his handkerchief, Andrew put it in his pocket and returned to the others. Though not as skillful as the gardener, Wyatt was young and strong and by now the hole was about four feet deep. Standing in it, he paused for a moment to wipe the perspiration from his face. As he picked up the shovel again, Ibrahim sighed and said, "Something is not right."

"What do you mean?" asked Finch.

"I was before sure there was body here. Now the *ka* or shadow of the *ka* is gone, and I am not sure. I go to temple to seek guidance and enlightenment." And bowing to the inspector, he walked off toward the grotto.

Finch stared after him, a vein in his forehead throbbing, then turned to Andrew and Sara. "Well?" he said with barely controlled rage, "have you changed your minds too?"

"About what?" asked Sara.

"About a body being buried here!"

"We never said the body was buried here," said Andrew. "We said that we saw a body that disappeared and that it was a logical deduction that it had been gotten over the wall somehow and—"

"Logical deduction?" roared Finch. "Nonsensical moonshine. I was an idiot to listen to you in the first place! I don't know what your game was, but I know there wasn't any murder, wasn't any body, and you should both get a good caning for having wasted so much of my time!"

"And who'd give it to us, you?" asked Sara, her eyes flashing and a good deal of her original Cockney creeping back into her speech. "You're right. You 'ave been an idiot—not because you listened to us, but because of the way you've gone about all this, calling people liars when they're not and trampling over clues like a blooming elephant!"

"Why, you little guttersnipe!" said Finch. He reached for her, but Wyatt, who had climbed out of the hole, pushed his hand away.

"All right, Finch," he said quietly but intensely. "That's enough!"

"What did you say?"

"I said that's enough!" repeated Wyatt, lifting him by the front of his jacket. "Sara's right, but she didn't go far enough. You've been acting, not just like an idiot, but like a boor and a bully as well—and it's time someone told you so. Not just told you, but—"

"Don't," said Andrew, putting his hand on Wyatt's arm. "It's not worth it."

"What?" said Wyatt.

"It isn't, really."

"No, perhaps not," said Wyatt, releasing the inspector. "Sorry."

"I'll wager you are!" said Finch, backing away from him. "But not nearly as sorry as you're going to be! You're going on report, my lad! And that's not all. I'm bringing you up on charges of insubordination and assaulting a superior officer. In the meantime, until the hearing, I'm relieving you of all duties and confining you to quarters. So go on back to the section-house and stay there!"

"Yes, sir," said Wyatt, his face expressionless. He started to march off, with Finch walking close behind him, then paused, said, "Excuse me, sir," and went back to get his helmet and tunic. As he bent down to pick them up, he whispered to Andrew and Sara, "Tell Beasley I want to see him right away. Tell him to come to the section-house."

They nodded and stood there as Wyatt went off toward the gate, followed by Finch.

9

The Watchers

They went to Portobello Road by omnibus. Andrew had plenty of money with him and was prepared to take a hansom or four-wheeler, but when they got to Wellington Road a dark green City Atlas bus came along and they took that to Oxford Street, changed there for a light green Bayswater.

Though, to begin with, they had been very upset at what had happened, they had been reassured by Wyatt's reaction to it. It was clear that he not only had no intention of letting Finch's attempt to discipline him keep him out of action, but that he had some plan in mind. The fact that he had given the two of them something to do helped even more. As a consequence, when they got off the bus at Pembridge Road, having ridden in the garden seat directly over the driver and behind the horses, they were almost cheerful.

It seemed that Portobello Road was not always as busy as it had been the day Wyatt took them there. On this particular day it was almost deserted, and Beasley was alone in his shop, studying a small stone statuette.

"It's you, eh?" he said, looking up at them with his baby blue eyes. "What's up?"

"It's Peter Wyatt," said Andrew. "He wants you to come see him right away."

"He does, eh? Where?"

"The section-house."

"Why the section-house?"

"Because he got into a shindy with Finch," said Sara. "Finch is going to bring him up on charges, whatever that is. And in the meantime he's supposed to stay in the section-house, not go anywhere."

"Friendship!" muttered Beasley, scowling. "Have you got any friends?" he asked Sara.

"A few."

"You?" he asked Andrew.

"One or two."

"Well, get rid of them! Having friends is one of the biggest mistakes you can make. In business, a yobbo comes to you with something like this," he held up the statuette, "and says, 'You can have it for a quid,' and if it's worth it, you take it. If not, you say no. But with friendship there's no figuring costs or convenience or anything. You come in and say, 'Wyatt wants you,' and

I'm supposed to drop everything and go running. Sean!" he called.

The curtain behind him was pulled aside and a slim, red-headed young man in his early twenties came out.

"Yes, Mr. Beasley?" he said with a slight Irish brogue.

"I'm going out. Watch the store."

"Yes, Mr. Beasley. What'll I tell Lamps about that?" he asked indicating the statuette.

"Andrew here's supposed to be a well-educated young man. Let's ask him. What do you think of it?" he asked Andrew.

Andrew had been looking at the statuette. It was about ten inches tall and it appeared to be a woman, though it was hard to tell, for though the figure was smooth and polished, it was very stylized and had almost no features.

"I don't know what it is, where it's from or anything about it," he said, "but I like it."

"You have good taste," said Beasley. "It's Cycladic, from one of the Greek islands, and probably dates from about 2500 B.C. The question is: Is it authentic or a fake?"

"I don't know."

"Well, I do," said Beasley. "Tell Lamps I'll give him ten bob for it because I like it, but that it's a fake. If he doesn't believe me, he can ask Gregorides at the British Museum." He rose. "Come on, you two," and he led the way out of the shop.

They went down the street together, Beasley walking quickly and with surprising lightness for such a large man. He let a hansom go by—it's doubtful whether anyone could have gotten into one with him—hailed a four-wheeler and told the cabby to take them to the police station on Wellington Road. When they were settled, Beasley on the rear seat and Sara and Andrew facing him, he said, "All right. Tell me what happened—everything that happened."

Sara began the story, with Andrew supplying a few additional details; and Andrew finished, with Sara supplying the details. Beasley closed his eyes and sat there quietly, remaining silent for several minutes even after they were done. Then, opening his eyes, he said, "I don't know Finch, don't know much about him, but what I do know, I don't like."

"Do you think he could have anything to do with what's been happening?" asked Sara. "The robberies and the murder?"

"No," said Beasley. "I think he's just a fool." He took a paper bag from one of the capacious pockets of his green velvet jacket and held it out to them. "Have an olive."

They were different from any olives Andrew had ever seen before: small, black and somewhat shrivelled, but when he ate one he liked it. Sara had taken one too but was looking at it suspiciously.

"What's an olive?" she asked.

Beasley groaned. "One of the oldest foods in the world," he said. "Older than cheese or wine, and probably older than bread, and she wants to know what it is. Eat it, and you'll see."

She put it in her mouth, chewed it slowly and thoughtfully, then said, "It's strange, but good."

They continued to eat the dried olives, spitting the pits out the window, until the four-wheeler drew up in front of the police station on Wellington Road.

"I don't know how long I'll be," said Beasley to the cabby as he got out, "but wait for me."

The cabby touched his hat with his whip.

"The two of you wait here also," said Beasley.

"Why can't we go in with you?" asked Sara.

"Because, if he's confined to quarters, it's going to be hard enough as it is to get them to let me see him. We'd never have a chance if we all went in." And squaring his shoulders, he marched up the three steps and into the police station. There was a two-story, frame building next to it. It was painted grey and looked institutional.

"Do you think that's the section-house?" asked Sara.

"It might be," said Andrew.

They tried peering through the windows. The first two looked into a large kitchen. The remaining one had opaque glass that they couldn't see through, and of course they couldn't look into the ones on the second story. They went around to the side of the building that was farthest from the police station. There was an open space that had been turned into a garden with flower beds edged with whitewashed stones on three sides and in the center a birdbath surrounded by a circle of gravel. As they walked around the garden, there was a sudden tapping, and looking up they saw Wyatt in one of the upstairs windows. He was in his shirt sleeves and he waved to them, gestured and then disappeared.

"He wants us to wait here," said Sara. "Do you think he's coming down?"

"I don't think he can," said Andrew. "But we'll see."

The door of the police station opened and Beasley came out looking bleak and angry.

"Sodding slops!" he said. "I never could stomach any of 'em except Wyatt! They won't let me see him."

"Why not?" asked Sara.

"Regulations. At least, that's what the sergeant said. (I'd like to regulate him with a shillelagh!) He's not supposed to see anyone *or* leave the section-house until his hearing. So I'm afraid that's that. I would have tried to do whatever he wanted if I'd known what it was, but . . ."

"He still may be able to tell us," said Andrew.

"How?"

"I'm not sure, but he was at that window a minute ago, and—Wait a minute. There he is again."

Wyatt had appeared at the window again with something in his hand. He opened the window, glanced around to make sure no one was watching, then tossed it out. Andrew caught it one-handed and saw that it was a cake of Pears Soap with a note wrapped around it. The note was addressed to Beasley, and Andrew gave it to him, looked up at the window again. Wyatt nodded his approval, shook a clenched fist, which probably indicated urgency, then closed the window and disappeared.

Meanwhile Beasley had unfolded the note. Both sides of the paper were covered with small, meticulous writing and as Beasley read it, he groaned.

"What is it?" asked Sara. "What's wrong?"

"Nothing," said Beasley, still reading. "Except that I wish I'd never gotten mixed-up with him. What does he think I am, anyway?"

"A friend," said Andrew.

"If I were half a dozen friends, I don't know how I'd be able to do all this," said Beasley, turning the note over.

"Anything we can do to help?" asked Sara.

"No," said Beasley. He turned back to the beginning of the note, then looked at them. "Are you far from home?"

"About a ten minute walk," said Andrew.

"Then I'll leave you here. I'd better get cracking." And he hurried to the waiting four-wheeler. "The nearest post office," he said, opening the door. "As quick as you can." He slammed the door, and the growler moved off into the traffic of Wellington Road.

Andrew and Sara watched him go.

"At least he might have told us what was in the note," said Sara.

"It was a pretty long one," said Andrew. "He must have had a lot of things to do."

"I know. Do you think we'll ever find out what was in it?"

"I expect so. Some day."

They walked home feeling, not just let down, but very much out of things. Verna was in her room, but when she heard them come in, she came down.

"You've been gone for quite a while," she said. "Were you over at Three Oaks all this time?"

"No," said Andrew. "We went to Portobello Road and then the police station on Wellington Road."

"Oh? What happened?"

They told her, not just what had happened at Three Oaks—the conflict between Wyatt and Finch and its result—but everything that had happened since. She was as good an audience as she was a performer and she listened intently but did not interrupt.

"You've no idea what Wyatt wanted this Beasley chap to do?" she asked.

"No. Though one of them was probably to send a telegram. That's why he went to the post office."

"Do you think it's concerned with the robberies and the murder, or the predicament he's in?"

"The robberies and the murder," said Sara. "I think

he knows or has figured out a lot more than he's told anyone, and the chief reason he's upset at what's happened to him is that it's keeping him from working on the case."

"And that's why you're upset too, isn't it?"

"What do you mean?" asked Andrew.

"He gave Beasley things to do, but not you. At least, not after you brought Beasley over there. However, I think that was very responsible of him. After all, it's not a game anymore. It's a very serious business, and you shouldn't be involved. As for those so-called charges against Wyatt, let's wait a few days and see what develops. If Finch has any sense, he'll forget about them. But if he doesn't, I'll see what I can do."

"Do you really think you can do something?" asked Andrew.

Verna shrugged. "One never knows till one tries. But since you won't be able to play detective, what are your plans for the afternoon?"

"I said something about taking Sara boating in Regent's Park."

"Splendid idea. It'll not only keep you out in the air, it'll keep your mind off other things."

Sara and Andrew looked at her to see if she was teasing them—which they wouldn't have liked—but, as was often the case with her, it was impossible to tell.

As was also often the case, there was a good deal in what Verna said. They did go to Regent's Park, and since Andrew handled a boat well and it was a beautiful day, they had a very good time. That, however, did not keep them from talking about Wyatt and wondering if they'd hear from him or Beasley. But there was no word from either of them that afternoon or that night.

Andrew first heard the sound of digging during break-fast the next morning, but he paid no attention to it. The streets of London were always being dug up for drains, gas mains, sewers, water pipes or, on a larger scale, for the Underground. But when he and Sara left the house later that morning they saw that the excavation was just up the road from their house and across the street from Three Oaks. That still meant nothing to them. They had decided that they would walk over to the section-house and see if they could catch a glimpse of Wyatt. perhaps even talk to him. But though they waited out-side for some time, there was no sign of him. When they returned to the house, they saw that some drain pipes had been delivered to the site of the excavation and that the two men who had been working there were putting up a fairly elaborate shelter with wooden sides and a canvas roof. Even this did not strike Andrew as strange, for though the excavation was still small, if it became large enough to require a watchman, why shouldn't he be protected from the weather?

Suddenly Andrew paused, and at that same moment, Sara, who was walking next to him, stopped also. One of the two men was of medium height but powerfully built, a typical navvy. The other was taller, slim and had red hair. Andrew and Sara looked at one another. They had both recognized him at the same time. He was Beasley's young shop assistant, Sean.

They walked toward him slowly. The navvy had picked up his shovel and was beginning to dig again. Sean drove a last nail into the shelter, then he saw them. His eyes widened, and he glanced at his companion. Then, looking at them again, he frowned and shook his head. The message was clear: go away, don't talk to me. Without a word they crossed the street and walked back toward the house.

"What's that all about?" asked Sara.

"I don't know," said Andrew. "At least, I'm not sure."

"It must have something to do with Wyatt's message to Beasley. I mean, Sean does work with him."

"Yes, he does."

That afternoon Verna took them to see Maskelyne and Cooke's Magic Show, which included some splendid conjuring and illusions like The Talking Head and The Disappearing Woman. Sara was one of those who accepted Maskelyne's invitation to come up on to the stage and see for themselves that there was no trickery involved when he levitated his female assistant and made her float in midair. And that, of course, made it an even more memorable occasion for Sara.

Verna was having dinner with Mr. Harrison, the theatre manager, and she sent Sara and Andrew home with Fred. After supper they played some parcheesi, but about eight thirty Andrew said, "I'd like some air. Do you feel like a walk?"

Sara looked at him, at her mother who was doing some mending while she watched them play, and said, "Yes, I would."

"It'll be dark soon," said Mrs. Wiggins. "Don't stay out too long."

"We won't, Mum," said Sara.

They went down the driveway, paused when they reached Rysdale Road.

"Where would you like to walk?" asked Andrew.

"Stop that," said Sara. "You know very well where."

He grinned, and together they crossed the street and walked toward the excavation. There had been no sign of activity there when they came home, and though all was still quiet now, there was a strong smell of tobacco in the air. Andrew lifted one side of the tarpaulin that served as a door for the shelter and there, sitting back in a comfortable chair and smoking a large cigar, was Beasley. Instead of his green velvet jacket, he now wore an old and ragged suit, a collarless shirt and a battered, broken-brimmed billycock hat.

"We thought we'd find you here," said Andrew.

"Did you?"

"Yes," said Sara. "What's the game?"

"Go away," said Beasley.

"That's what Sean wanted us to do this morning," said

Andrew. "Go away and not ask questions. Well, we're not going until you tell us what you're doing."

"I'm not doing anything," said Beasley. "Business at the shop's been bad. That's why I took this job here."

"What job?" asked Sara.

"Night watchman. Nothing wrong with that, is there? Or strange or mysterious?"

"No," said Andrew. "Though I'd like to know what you're watching."

Beasley, who had been lounging back in his chair, leaned forward.

"Is Wyatt a friend of yours?" he asked. "Do you want to help him?"

"Yes," said Andrew.

"Then go away and stay away! Don't come back here and stop asking questions!"

"Righto, mate," said Sara. "You've told us what we wanted to know." And she and Andrew backed out and let the tarpaulin fall back into place again.

"It's Three Oaks he's watching, isn't it?" asked Sara.

"It must be," said Andrew. "No matter what Finch thought, Wyatt thinks there's something funny going on there, so he asked Beasley to keep an eye on it for him."

"I wonder what he expects to happen."

"I don't know, but it means he hasn't given up. That even though he can't leave the section-house, he's still thinking about the case, trying to do something about it."

"I wish we could help him."

"So do I, but you heard what Beasley said. That if we did want to help we should stay away."

"Yes," said Sara without much enthusiasm or conviction.

Andrew had a strange dream that night. He dreamed that he and Sara were at the Olympia again; not with Wyatt but alone, and not in the amphitheatre but in one of the corridors outside. A performance was in progress—they could hear the music of the band, the thunder of galloping hoofs and the applause of the crowd—but they couldn't go in. Instead they kept wandering unhappily up one dismal corridor and down another with the conviction that there was something they should be doing—something very important—but with no idea of what it was.

It was while he was dressing the next morning that the answer came to him. He hurried downstairs, found that early as it was Sara had already had breakfast with her mother. She followed him into the breakfast room, however, and when they were alone and the door was carefully closed, Andrew said, "I've been thinking. We're pretty sure that the reason Sean and Beasley are up the street, posing as a navvy and a night watchman, is that they want to watch Three Oaks." Sara nodded. "Beasley told us if we want to help we should stay away, so we will. But there's no reason why we shouldn't watch too—from here. I can see part of the grounds from my room, so if we go up higher, we should be able to see even more."

Sara's face lit up. "I know just the place."

"Where?"

"Finish your breakfast and I'll show you."

He ate quickly, followed her out and up the stairs. The servants' rooms were on the top floor but that couldn't be what she had in mind because they couldn't watch from one of them without having all sorts of questions asked. And it couldn't be the box room, which took up the rear half of the top floor, because its only window faced the wrong way, away from Three Oaks.

When they reached the top floor, however, Sara opened a door next to the box room, one that Andrew had always thought led to a closet because Annie kept some of her mops and pails there. Andrew followed her inside, she closed the door, and now he saw that behind the door there was a ladder that led up to a trapdoor in the ceiling.

"What's up there?" he asked.

"Go up and see."

He climbed the ladder, lifted the trapdoor and found himself in the space between the ceilings of the servants rooms and the box room and the roof beams. It ran the length of the house from front to back, was about four feet high in the center and lower on the sides where the roof sloped down. The reason Sara had led him there was right in front of him; a dormer window that faced Three Oaks.

"How did you find it?" he asked Sara, who had come up the ladder behind him.

She shrugged. "I had lots of time to explore while you were away at school. What do you think?"

He kneeled down and looked out of the window. From it he could see not only most of the grounds and the house itself but the shelter next to the excavation across the road.

"It's perfect. We can not only watch Three Oaks, but Beasley too."

"That's what I thought. When shall we start?"

"There's not much point in watching during the day. I don't think anything will happen then, and besides someone might see us and ask what we're doing. But we can start tonight."

"And watch all night?"

"Don't you think we could if we took turns?"

"Yes. Let's try anyway."

They had gone somewhere or done something every day since Andrew had come home—it's what people expected you to do during a holiday—and they felt they should continue the pattern. After some discussion they went to the British Museum, and even though they had things on their mind, they enjoyed the afternoon; Andrew because he'd only been there once before, and Sara because she'd been there several times with Miss

Poole and the girls from her class at school and she liked
the idea of going to a place she was more familiar with
than he. They spent some time in the Greek Rooms, particularly the one containing the Elgin Marbles, and the
rest of the time in the Egyptian Rooms, where they came
on a guide who was explaining the importance of the
Rosetta Stone to a mixed group of tourists. They had
tea in the Refreshment Room opposite the Central Egyptian Saloon and took a bus home.

Beasley took out a cigar, looked at it regretfully, then
put it away. Sean had insisted that it was out of charac-
ter; that if a night watchman smoked anything, it would
be an old pipe and had given him the dudeen he'd
been smoking during the day. It was next to him now,
lying on the crate Beasley used as a table, with a package
of cheap shag, but remembering the way it smelled, he
decided not to smoke at all for the moment. He got up,
pushed aside the tarpaulin and stepped outside.

It was a warm night, overcast and therefore quite dark.
The clock on the church on Wellington Road chimed
once. That made it a quarter after nine—which meant
that most of the night was still ahead of him. He groaned
softly, wishing he'd never met Peter Wyatt. There were
footsteps behind him. He turned, and by the yellow glow
of the gaslight further up the street, he saw a small, clean-
shaven, neatly dressed man in a bowler coming towards
him.

"Good evening," said the man.

"Evening."

"Nice night."

"Nice enough. But warm."

"It is that. My name's Potter. I'm Mr. Fulton's man."

"Who?"

"Mr. Fulton." He nodded towards the villa just up the street. "It's our drain you're replacing. At least . . . isn't it?"

"I'd be the last to know, mate."

"How's that?"

"Because that's the way it is. Young Alf, who took my niece Maggie for better or worse, he's the contractor, see? He stops by and says, 'Unk, I got a job for you. Be at Rysdale Road at seven tonight.' So up I toddle and there's the job and I know what I gotta do—keep an eye on things—but who it's for I never know."

"I see. I wondered because it all seemed very casual. I'm on my way to *The Red Lion*, our local. This is a very safe neighborhood and I'm sure if you were to slip away, come there with me for a while . . ."

"Couldn't," said Beasley. "Thanks, but t'wouldn't be right."

"I must say that's very responsible of you. I don't expect to stay very long—I'll just have a pint or two. Can I bring you anything on my way back?"

A pint. Beasley was always as thirsty as he was hungry, and his adam's apple did a quick up and down at the thought of a cool pint. But . . .

"Much obleeged," he said. "But I'd better not. I have enough trouble staying awake as it is. And since this is only my second night here and Alfie could stop by to check up on me . . ."

"I understand," said Potter. "But that's easy. There's a coffee stall just across the street from the pub. I'd be glad to bring you a cup on my way home."

"That's something I wouldn't say no to."

"I'll see you later, then, a little before closing time." And with a nod and a smile he walked off toward Wellington Road.

Sara woke Andrew at about twelve thirty. Since Verna usually looked in on Andrew when she came home from the theatre, sat and talked to him for a few minutes if he was awake, they thought it would be best if Sara took the first watch. Andrew had gone up with her, stayed until a little after ten, then gone down again so as to be certain he was in his room when Verna came home. He was sure he wouldn't sleep—he was much too excited—just thought it would look better if he were in bed . . . and the next thing he knew Sara was shaking him.

He sat up with a start, and Sara put her hand over his mouth to keep him from saying anything. When she was sure he was awake, she removed it.

"Is she home?" he whispered.

"She came home about a half-hour ago."

He got out of bed, put on his robe and slippers, tip-toed to the door and opened it slightly. There was no sign of a light in Verna's room.

"All right," he whispered. "I'll go up. You go to bed." He started up the stairs, paused when he saw that she was following him. "Where are you going?"

"With you. I'm not sleepy. I'll stay with you for a while the way you did with me."

He hesitated, then shrugged and continued up the stairs. Matson's room was dark also—he must have gone to bed right after he let Verna in—but they were quiet anyway as they crept past it. Andrew had oiled the hinges of the closet door so it opened noiselessly. They went in, up the ladder, and then they were in their eyrie.

"You're sure you want to do this?" Andrew asked.

"Yes."

"Stretch out on this, then." He pulled over the old blanket they had brought up earlier. Sara made herself comfortable, folding one end of the blanket over as a pillow while Andrew sat down next to the window.

"You didn't see anything at all during your watch?"

"Nothing important. A man came by and gave Beasley a cup of coffee or tea."

"Sean?"

"No. A small man wearing a bowler. He went on up the street."

"He probably lives somewhere around here."

"Probably. Do you think something's going to happen, Andrew?"

"I don't know. Wyatt must think so or he wouldn't have asked Beasley to keep an eye out. But that doesn't mean it'll happen tonight."

"I know." She was quiet for several minutes. "Do you remember that book you read to me when you first stayed with us at Dingell's Court—Sam's book?"

"That penny-dreadful, *The Boy Detective?*"

"Yes. Well, in a way, that's what we are now, isn't it?"

He smiled. "You mean the boy and the girl detective?"

"Are there such things as girl detectives—lady detectives?"

"I've never heard of any, but I'm sure there will be some day—if any ladies want to be detectives."

"I'd rather be an actress like your mother. But I'd like to help Peter Wyatt become one. *And* I'd like to do Finch in the eye by finding that body he says we didn't see. And most of all, I'd like to get back those diamonds that were taken from your mum."

"I'd like all that too, particularly helping Wyatt. It doesn't seem right that he shouldn't be able to become a detective when it's what he wants to do."

"Especially when we know he'd be a very good one. Because I think he would be, don't you?"

"Yes, I do."

He thought about that; about what made people decide what they wanted to do or be. In most cases there wasn't much choice. Take the two boys he'd travelled down from school with. Bragaw was going to be a barrister because that's what his father was. And Chadwick thought he'd go into the diplomatic service because his father was in the Foreign Office. Which made Andrew admire Wyatt all the more for refusing to go into the army like his father and brothers, partly because he wanted to be a detective and partly because he was determined to be his own man.

He started to say something about this to Sara, noticed that her eyes were closing. She forced them open, looked at him without really seeing him, then turned on her side and fell fast asleep. Andrew looked at her thoughtfully, decided it was better to let her sleep where she was than wake her and get her down to her own room. Making himself comfortable, he settled down to his watch.

There was, he discovered, a big difference between what he had been able to see that morning and what he could see now. That morning he had not only been able to see all of Three Oaks from the house to the surrounding wall, he had been able to distinguish most of its physical features; tell the fruit trees from the shade trees, the formal flower beds from the rock garden. Now all he could see were darker or less dark masses, with the house, faintly visible against the sky, the darkest mass of all. Rysdale Road was a little better; the streetlight just beyond Beasley's shelter on the far side of the street

ngreased wheel. Then suddenly there

id Sara. Her eyes widened. "Andrew,
can have anything to do with what's
ere?"

pped somewhere this side of the gate."
back inside Three Oaks. They could still
suddenly, for the first time, they heard
sound of footsteps on gravel. The two,
were, had come down to the walk just
. Then, with no warning, a light flashed,
e shrubbery to the wall, then disappeared
realized later that the two night-walkers
n carrying bull's-eye lanterns, opened, then
utters.) In that momentary gleam of light
ot see the mysterious two, but they could
y had been moving so slowly and carefully.
carrying something; a rectangular black
more than six feet long.
!" said Andrew. "I think . . . Brother Ibra-
!"

how what's in it, don't you?" said Sara. "A
nge to all of Lombard Street it's the stiff that
ed!"

bly. And now they're going to get rid of it.
hat the dray's waiting for!"
ou think Beasley knows?"
ust!"

and another one farther up the road on the near side helped illuminate it. This could well be important, but at the moment, it didn't matter very much because there was no sign of movement in the part he could see: no hansom or four-wheeler went either up it or down it nor were there any belated pedestrians.

Andrew tried to divide his time equally between the grounds and the street outside, watching one for a while, then switching to the other. The night was still as well as dark. Not a leaf stirred either inside or outside Three Oaks and the only sound was Sara's regular, quiet breathing. Time passed. And suddenly he realized he had been looking at one tree for some time—looking at it but not really seeing it—and he also realized that his eyes were starting to close as Sara's had. He shook his head to clear it. He mustn't fall asleep now—he couldn't! He started reciting poetry to himself—all the poems he could remember—to help keep awake. He ran through several ballads and was on *Kubla Khan*, one of his favorites, when his eyes closed again.

He did not know how long he slept or what woke him—possibly the chime on the church clock because, as he opened his eyes, he heard the grandfather clock, which was a minute or two slow, striking on the landing two floors below him. It seemed to have struck only once. Did that mean it was one o'clock? Or was it a quarter after one or two or even three?

He turned to look at Sara. She had not moved, was

lying on her side, eyes closed, breathing softly and regularly. He looked out the window again—at Three Oaks first—and stiffened. There was a change here, possibly a significant one. A light was on now in one of the bedrooms. Of course, he did not know how long it had been on or what it meant. Possibly someone had awakened and, unable to fall asleep again, had lit one of the gas jets. On the other hand . . .

No! It was more than that—it had to be—for there were now two more lights! They were rather faint and while one of them was stationary, the other was moving slowly down through the grounds toward it. Andrew watched them for a moment, then shook Sara gently. Her eyes opened. She looked at him, around the dark attic, then sat up.

"What is it?" she whispered.

He nodded toward the window, and she moved closer to him and looked out.

"Lights," she said. "I don't know where that one is, but the other's coming down from the house."

"I think the first one's somewhere near the greenhouse," said Andrew.

She studied the stationary light. "I think you're right. But who can they be and what are they doing?"

"I don't know who, but they're obviously meeting. There!"

The moving light reached the other, then they both went out.

"Then where is he?"

"In the shelter. That's why they put it up, so he could keep out of sight. What do you expect him to do, dance a war dance in the middle of Rysdale Road?"

"No, but . . . suppose he fell asleep?"

"I guess he could. I did myself a little while ago. Perhaps we should go see."

Sara nodded, and they lifted the trapdoor, hurried down the ladder and the stairs. When they were on the floor below, Andrew, remembering how he'd gone look-ing for a policeman in his slippers, said, "This time I'm going to get dressed."

"Is there time?"

"They still have to get the coffin over the wall."

"Then I'll get dressed, too. Meet you downstairs."

Andrew ran into his room, pulled his shirt and trousers on over his pajamas, stepped into his boots, and then was on his way downstairs. He had just opened the front door when Sara came down. They ran down the driveway together, paused when they came to the street, looking to the left. The dray was still there, just past the street-light. They ran across the street on tiptoe, pulled aside the tarpaulin that covered the entrance and froze. Beasley was leaning back in his chair, mouth open and eyes closed, snoring like a laboring locomotive.

"He *is* asleep!" said Sara. She took him by the arm and shook him violently. "Baron, wake up!"

Beasley didn't move. His eyes didn't open, and there

was no change in the timbre of his snoring.

"Baron!" said Sara, shaking him even harder. Eyes still closed, Beasley slid off the chair to the floor, continued snoring. Sara looked down at him with shocked amazement, then looked at Andrew. "What's wrong with him?"

Andrew picked up a thick china mug from the crate next to the chair, looked into it, smelled it and grimaced.

"He's not asleep," he said. "He's been drugged."

10

The Chase

"Who drugged him?" asked Sara.

"Someone who didn't want him to see what we saw—what's going on now. Didn't you say a man in a bowler brought him a cup of coffee or tea?"

"Yes. What shall we do? Get the police?"

"We don't have the time. Besides, even if we found a constable right away, he probably wouldn't believe us."

"No. Wyatt's the only one who would, and . . ."

"I'm going to get him."

"Wyatt? He's not supposed to leave the section-house."

"When he hears what's happening, he will."

"But you said yourself we don't have much time, and he's all the way over on Wellington Road."

"I said I'd get him, and I will. Can you see the dray from here?"

Sara found a crack in the wooden sides of the shelter and peered out.

"Yes."

"Good. Then stay here and keep your eye on it. If we're not back in time, see which way it goes. But don't do anything foolish!"

"I won't."

"Promise?"

"Yes."

"Good." He squeezed her arm, lifted the tarpaulin and peered out. The dray was some distance up the street and the man and woman on the box could not see him, but he was still careful. He crouched low as he ran across the road to the driveway, kept to the grass as he went up toward the house, then cut around behind it to the stable. He slid the stable door open as quietly as he could. A lantern hung from an overhead beam, and he knew where Fred kept the matches. He struck one, lit the lantern. The bay carriage horses were in the first two stalls, the grey hunter in the third. All three of them looked at him. He ran back to the hunter, untied his halter and backed him out. The grey nuzzled him, looking for the carrot or apple that Andrew usually gave him.

"Later," said Andrew softly.

He took down the bridle, took off the halter, slipped the bit into the grey's mouth and buckled it. His first thought had been to have Fred take him over to the section-house. But when he thought of having to wake him, explain where he wanted to go and why, he knew it was impossible. The one thing he wasn't sure about was whether he'd have trouble putting a bridle on the hunter. He didn't—and he wasn't going to bother with a saddle—so that was that.

He turned the horse, but as he started to lead him out, there was a sudden thump in the room above the stable where Fred slept and the door at the top of the stairs opened.

"Wazzat?" asked Fred, still half-asleep. "Who's that down there?"

"It's all right, Fred. It's me, Andrew. I'm taking the hunter."

"You're what?"

"Taking the hunter." He climbed on to a box and from there onto the hunter's back. "I'll explain later."

"Are you off your everlasting chump?" Fred, in night cap and night shirt, started down the stairs. Then as Andrew shook the reins and cantered out of the stable, "Hi! Come back here!"

Anxious to make as little noise as possible, Andrew held the grey in and rode across the lawn instead of down the driveway. Reaching Rysdale Road, he turned right and continued to hold him in until he was some distance up the street. Then, leaning forward, he gave the horse his head, urging him on. The grey, always eager for a run, went into a long-striding canter and then into a gallop. Andrew found that there was a big difference between riding bareback when the horse was walking in the yard and when he was galloping up the street. But gripping with his knees, he not only stayed on but began to enjoy himself. It was very exciting to be racing up Rysdale Road at night like one of the Indians in the Wild West Show, especially when it was on such an important mission.

Reaching Wellington Road, he turned right. He had seen no one so far, saw no one now as he rode north on Wellington Road; no pedestrians, hansoms, growlers or carriages. There were no lights on in either the police station or the section-house. Riding into the garden next to the section-house, Andrew pulled up, slipped off the hunter's back and, tying him to the bird bath, picked up a handful of gravel and threw it at the middle, second-floor window; the one at which he and Sara had seen Wyatt.

For a moment nothing happened. He had thought ahead this far, but no farther. What would he do if he couldn't wake Wyatt or if he had been sent somewhere else and was no longer there? Should he go into the section-house and wake someone else? If he felt he didn't have time enough to tell Fred where he wanted to go and why, what chance did he have of getting a suddenly awakened policeman to come back to Rysdale Road with him before the dray left? Then the window opened, and Wyatt was looking out.

"You!" he said, surprised. "What's up?"

"Something going on at Three Oaks."

"Oh?" Though he had been surprised to see Andrew there, he did not seem surprised at that. "Be with you in a minute."

He left the window open, disappeared. He had apparently been sleeping in his shirt and trousers. A moment later a rope came flying out, and Wyatt, fully dressed, followed it and slid down the rope to the ground.

"Will your horse carry double?" he asked.

"I think so."

"All right. Up you get." He lifted Andrew on to the grey's back, swung up behind him. "Keep to a canter—I don't know if I can stay on in a gallop—and tell me about it as we go."

Andrew turned the hunter, shook the reins and as he went back down Wellington Road at a slow, rocking canter, he told Wyatt everything that had happened, everything he and Sara had seen. Holding onto him, Wyatt listened quietly, asked only one question.

"You're sure that Beasley was drugged? That he wasn't hurt?"

"Fairly sure. There was some white powder left in his cup, and he seemed to be in a deep, heavy sleep."

"Good. Poor Baron. None of this was his dish. But it certainly seems to be yours. I don't know what I'd have done without you and Sara."

Andrew flushed with pleasure. "We haven't gotten

anybody yet, either the murderer or the thief who stole all the jewels."

"No, we haven't. But if we do, it will be in large part because of the two of you."

"Is it the same person—the murderer and the thief?"

"In a way, yes. And in a way, no. One man—the man who committed the murder—is responsible for everything that happened even though he didn't do all the stealing."

"And you know who he is?"

"I'm not sure I can prove it, but I think so." They had turned into Rysdale Road now, were cantering up it. "Easy now. Where's the dray?"

"Up ahead there."

"Where?"

Andrew peered through the darkness towards the distant streetlight.

"It's gone!" he said. "We're too late."

"I was afraid of that," said Wyatt. "I'm sure no one could have been quicker than you, but you not only had to get the horse, you had a long way to go after that. But Sara should at least be able to tell us which way they went. She's in the shelter?"

"Yes," said Andrew unhappily.

Wyatt dismounted, lifted the tarpaulin and looked into the shelter.

"No, she's not. She's gone too."

"What?" Andrew jumped off the hunter and looked into the shelter also. Beasley, breathing heavily, lay on

the ground where Andrew had last seen him, but there was no sign of Sara.

"You've no idea where she might have gone?" asked Wyatt.

"No. She promised she'd stay here, wouldn't do anything foolish."

"Well, it's my impression that she's a pretty level-headed girl. Do you think she might have gone back to the house?"

"It's possible, but I don't think so. I think she'd rather wait here for us than wake anyone in the house."

Wyatt nodded. "Show me where the dray was waiting."

Leading the hunter, Andrew went up the street almost to the streetlight.

"It was just about here," he said. "It—" He broke off. There was a small pile of oats a few feet from the curb and, leading away from it and up the street was a faint, but regular trail.

"Did you happen to notice if there was a bag of oats on the dray?" asked Wyatt.

"Yes. There was a feed bag hanging from the rear axle."

"Then she either made a hole in it or . . ." He hesitated.

"Or she climbed on the back and is dropping the oats. And if I know her, that's what she did. Come on."

He pulled on the hunter's reins, but before he could

mount there was the sound of horses' hoofs and wheels on gravel and the landau came rattling down the driveway and out into the road with Fred in the box.

"So there you are," he said to Andrew as he pulled up. "I wasn't sure how far I'd have to chase you or what your game was. But now that I see *you* here . . ." he said to Wyatt. "What's up?"

"A very rum go at Three Oaks. A man I think is a murderer came over the wall and went off in a dray. Sara was watching, and we're fairly sure she hooked a ride on it and is leaving that trail of oats for us."

"Well, what are you waiting for?" said Fred. "Come on up, then."

"Right," said Wyatt, climbing up next to him.

"I'll ride," said Andrew, swinging up on to the grey's back. "I'll be able to see better that way." And leaning down as far as he dared, he sent the hunter trotting up the road. Luckily there was still no wind, and even though the streetlights were widely separated, the trail of oats was undisturbed and fairly easy to follow. It turned south at the corner and following it, Andrew looked back and saw the landau coming after him. Since the trail seemed to be going straight ahead, he sat up, putting the hunter into a canter. A few minutes later they reached Prince Albert Road, crossed the Regent's Canal and turned east on the Outer Circle of Regent's Park. The streetlights were spaced further apart here and the trail harder to see and follow. Then suddenly it

stopped. Andrew reined in the hunter, bent down again, peering through the darkness. He still couldn't find the trail of oats, and he was about to dismount and search for it on foot when the landau pulled up beside him.

"There it is," said Wyatt, pointing. "At least . . . Isn't that it?"

Andrew looked where he was pointing. There, on the lawn between the Outer Circle and the canal, faintly visible against the gaslights of Prince Albert Road, was the dray. The horse that had pulled it was tied to a bush near the canal and, head down, was grazing peacefully.

"Yes!" said Andrew.

"Wait a minute," said Wyatt as Andrew turned the hunter. But he didn't wait, galloped across the lawn to the dray. The dray horse lifted his head and whinnied as Andrew dismounted, then went on grazing.

Holding the hunter's reins, Andrew saw that his fears were justified. There was no sign of the man who had been driving the dray, of the old woman who had been with him, or—most important—of Sara. He looked into the canvas-covered back of the dray. Nothing. He had been concerned enough, anxious enough before. Now he was really frightened. As he started to walk around to the front of the dray, Wyatt came running up.

"Where's Sara?" he asked.

"I don't know. Do you think they found her and took her off someplace?"

"No. We agreed that she was a sensible girl and you

say that she promised you that she wouldn't do anything foolish . . ."

"And what do you call what she did, hooking a ride on the back of the dray?"

"I'll admit I'm not too happy about it," said Wyatt—and Andrew suddenly realized that he was just as worried as Andrew was. "But—"

He broke off as Fred, still sitting in the box of the landau, whistled shrilly and pointed. They turned—and trudging slowly toward them along the edge of the canal, was Sara.

They hurried toward her.

"Are you all right?" asked Andrew.

"What?" said Sara unhappily. "Yes, of course I'm all right. But we lost them. They got away."

"Who, Sara?" asked Wyatt. "Could you tell?"

"Yes. A small man—the man who gave Beasley the cup of coffee. I didn't recognize him at first because he wore a bowler then, and a cap when he was driving the dray. And an old woman that Andrew and I both thought looked familiar. And someone else, a man in a cape."

"You don't know who he was?"

"No. He had his collar up and a hat pulled down so I couldn't see his face."

"Did he come from Three Oaks?"

"Yes. The man on the dray threw a rope over the wall. That's how they got the coffin out."

"Brother Ibrahim's coffin?"

"Yes. Then the man in the cape came over the wall, the three of them put the coffin in the back of the dray, they all got in front and drove off."

"And you went with them," said Andrew sternly.

"Well, yes. I kept looking up the street for some sign of you, but there wasn't any so, when they started, I ran after them and got on behind—I used to do that lots when we lived at Dingell's Court. At the same time, I grabbed the feed bag and kept dropping handfuls of oats. That's how you followed us, isn't it?"

"Yes," said Wyatt. "That was very clever of you."

"Even if it was, what good did it do? I told you, they got away."

"How, Sara?" asked Andrew.

"There was a tugboat waiting there." She pointed at the canal. "I jumped off and hid in the bushes when they stopped. They carried the coffin to the tug, got on and went off."

"Which way?" asked Wyatt.

"That way," she said, pointing east.

"Did you see the name of the tug, by any chance?"

"Yes. The *Harrier* of Greenwich."

"Good work. Come on." He started back toward the landau. "If we're lucky, we can still catch them."

"You really think so?"

"Yes. This was all carefully planned. They've undoubtedly made arrangements to board a ship somewhere in the lower Thames—Gravesend or Tilbury. But first they've got to get there. We'll see if we can't cut them off."

"Somewhere on the canal?" asked Andrew.

"No. It goes into a tunnel just this side of Islington and we couldn't get to them. But they'll come out into the Thames at Limehouse, and we'll try and catch them somewhere between there and their ship."

"We'll need a fast boat for that," said Sara. "The tug went off like a scalded cat."

"There aren't many faster boats on the Thames than a river police launch."

They were back at the landau, and hearing that, Fred didn't have to hear any more.

"Is that what we want now?" he asked. "The river police?"

"Yes. Their headquarters is on High Street in Wapping. Do you know where that is?"

"Can a fish swim? Get in." He looked at Andrew as Sara and Wyatt climbed up into the box with him. "Do you want to tie the hunter on in back and get in too?"

"No. I'll ride and follow you."

"That's what you've been waiting for, isn't it? To ride bareback through London like a naked red Indian. Well, I hope you can stick it because I'm going to be clipping."

It may or may not have been what Andrew wanted, but it was clear that after having driven the bays sedately for so long, Fred was delighted to have an excuse to let them out. He cracked his whip over their heads, putting them first into a trot and then into a gallop. Andrew followed, and it was a ride he would never forget, for with half of London to cross, Fred kept up the pace he had set and Andrew was hard-pressed to stay with him.

They went round the Outer Circle, leaving the park after they'd passed St. Katherine's Hospital and from that point on going always east and south, first heading toward the river along Tottenham Court Road, then going east along High Holborn, clattering over the Holborn Viaduct and along Newgate Street. It was almost five o'clock when they reached St. Paul's, and in the early morning light Andrew could see the domed bulk of the cathedral to his right as they went by. From Cheapside, Fred cut over to Cannon Street, around the Monument and up Eastcheap and Great Tower Street to Tower Hill, thus avoiding Lower Thames Street and the Billingsgate Market. However, they were close enough to it so that now, for the first time, they began to run into traffic and had to cut around drays, carts and vans, whose drivers looked after them in surprise, hailing them and shouting questions after them, for it was not a common thing to see a landau driven hell-for-leather through the narrow streets of the City at that hour of the morning, especially when it was closely followed by a boy riding bareback.

The horses were laboring a bit when they got to the top of Tower Hill, and Fred eased up a little. By now it was light enough so that Andrew could see the high, crenellated walls of the Tower to his right.

They went around it, past the Royal Mint and then plunged down into a world of docks that was completely strange to Andrew, and through which he could never have found his way, past the vast basin of St. Katherine's Docks, the wharfs, warehouses and sheds that surrounded it, over to Wapping High Street, which ran alongside the river, finally stopping before a brick building with a green light on each side of the door and a sign over it that said, Headquarters, Thames Police.

"Here y'are," said Fred, clearly pleased with himself.

"Well done," said Wyatt, jumping down. "I hope I do half as well." Then, misquoting slightly, "If you have prayers, prepare to say them now."

"Why?" asked Sara. "Do you expect to have trouble in there?"

"Yes. The Thames Police are pretty independent anyway, and I'm only a constable. It usually takes an order direct from Scotland Yard to get them to do anything. But we'll see." And he hurried into the building.

Andrew, stiff and a little sore from his ride, slipped down off the hunter and stood there for a moment, trying to relax his aching muscles.

"Well, Buffalo Bill, how's your back?" asked Fred.

"Not too bad."

"You did pretty well. I wasn't sure you could stay on, much less keep up with us all that road."

"Neither was I," said Andrew. Then to Sara, "Shall we go in too?"

"He didn't say we shouldn't."

"Go ahead," said Fred. "I'll watch the horses."

"Thanks, Fred," said Andrew, and helping Sara down, they went into the building.

Wyatt was standing in front of the desk, talking to a burly grey-haired man with a walrus mustache, who was looking anything but sympathetic and responsive.

"Who are these two?" he asked when Sara and Andrew came in.

"Friends of mine," said Wyatt. "They kept watch on the gang we're after, sent me word when they scarpered."

"And what are you after this gang for?"

"Robbery and murder."

"Well, that's serious enough, but you're going about it all vicey-versy. You say Inspector Finch is in charge of the case?"

"Yes."

"Well, the request should come from him. I'll tell you what. I'll telegraph the Yard and leave word for him. And when he comes in, he can get back to me, and—"

"But don't you understand that there's no time for that?" said Wyatt. "There's no telling when he'll get to the Yard, and in the meantime the people we want are on a tug coming down the canal. Once they reach the Thames, we'll never catch them!"

"I wouldn't say that. There aren't many boats on the river that can show their heels to our launches." It was clear that, in spite of himself, he was becoming intrigued. "Wanted for murder, eh?"

"Yes. And some of the most important robberies we've had in years. The Denham diamonds among other things."

"Oh? We got a flyer on that the other day. Stolen from an actress, weren't they?"

"Yes. His mother, Verna Tillett," said Sara, indicating Andrew. "Will you tell me something. Do you think Constable Wyatt's lying? That there is no gang?"

"Well, no. There'd be no point in his lying about it. But there's a right and a wrong way to go about these things."

"And is it the right way to let them get away because we can't get hold of Finch? I wonder what Superintendent Wendell's going to say about that."

"Superintendent Wendell? Is he in on the case, too?"

"He's very interested in it," said Wyatt.

The grey-haired man grunted, looked sharply at Wyatt, at Sara and Andrew, then called, "Robbie!"

A younger man, wearing the shiny black boater that was the official headgear of the Thames police, came in and saluted.

"Is there steam up in the launch?" asked the grey-haired man.

"Yes, Inspector."

"Good. We're going out. You go ahead with Robbie," he said to Wyatt. "We won't wait for Finch, but I think we should notify him."

"Of course," said Wyatt. He glanced at Sara and Andrew and said, "Can they come with us? Sara was the one who saw them board the tug, and she'll be able to recognize it."

"If you know the name, there shouldn't be any trick to that, but . . . since we're not doing any of this according to Cocker, why not?" and he went off to put a message on the A.B.C. of the official circuit.

"Thanks," said Andrew to Wyatt.

"You're a wonder!" said Sara, her eyes bright.

"No, you are," said Wyatt. "You're the one who got him to do it. But we'd better tell Fred what's on."

They found him tying the hunter to the back of the landau. He listened to what they had to say and nodded.

"I was sure you'd work it somehow. Don't worry about the hunter. I'll lead him back. And of course, I'll tell your two mums where you are and what you're up to." He climbed up into the box. "And tally-blooming-ho! Good hunting!"

They went back into headquarters, out a door on the far side and down the slippery wooden steps to the floating dock. The rakish black steam launch with her single tall smokestack was tied there, her engine already throbbing. The constable, Robbie, was forward at the lines, and there was a man below, tending the engine.

As they boarded the launch, the grey-haired man with the mustache, Inspector Thatcher, came nimbly down the steps. He was wearing a shiny black hat now too.

"If this is as big a thing as you say," he said, jumping aboard, "I want to be in on it. All right, Robbie. Cast off." He took the tiller, and as Robbie cast off the lines he guided the launch away from the dock and out into the stream. "What time did the tug start down the canal?"

"A little before four," said Wyatt.

"She won't have reached the river yet, and we haven't far to go. We'll be waiting for them when they come out of the basin."

The sun was rising dead ahead of them, showing the cranes of the West India Docks and the masts and spars of the ships that were tied up there in stark silhouette. Keeping to the middle of the river to take advantage of the current, Thatcher talked to them about what they were seeing. The part of the river they were in now—the section between London Bridge and Limehouse Reach, where the river curves south and then north again around the Isle of Dogs—was called The Pool. Directly below them, deep under the brown, fast-moving water, was the Thames Tunnel that connected Wapping on the east bank with Rotherhithe on the south.

He continued with his description as they went downstream, finally pointing to a series of quays to their left and saying, "There we are."

"Is that the entrance to the canal?" asked Wyatt.

"To the Limehouse Basin, which leads into both the Regent's Canal and the Limehouse Cut, which connects with the River Lea."

"Is this the only place the tug can come out then?" asked Sara.

"Well, no," said the inspector slowly. "They could take the Cut to the Lea and then come down Bow Creek. That would take them out into the river farther down, on the other side of the East India Docks. But this is the easiest, the most direct way."

"So what it comes down to is whether they knew— or suspected—that anyone was following them. What do you think?" Wyatt asked Sara and Andrew.

They looked at one another. "There was no way they could have known up to the time I left to get you," said Andrew slowly. "After that . . . What do you think, Sara?"

She thought about it even more carefully than Andrew had. Finally she shook her head.

"No. I don't think they knew."

"All right," said Wyatt. "I'll say that it's a good bet that they don't know and that they'll come out here. What do we do?"

"Wait," said Thatcher.

Putting up the tiller, he eased the launch alongside a pile a few hundred yards upstream from the entrance to the basin. Robbie tied her there, and in silence and with some uneasiness—for how could they be sure that they were not mistaken?—they settled down to wait.

It was still very early, probably not yet six o'clock, but there was already a good deal of activity on the river. A Thames barge, brown topsail and mainsail spread wide, came down the river. A paddlewheel steamer, coming up, blew a single blast on its whistle and gave it right of way. A huge, black, gaff-rigged sail appeared above the stone quays at the entrance to the basin, and a wherry came sailing out and crossed the river toward Rotherhithe. The funnel of a tugboat, clearly laboring, appeared at the entrance to the basin. When it came out into the stream they saw that it was towing four barges. It swung around, started moving slowly upstream against the current, passing so close to them that they could almost count the bricks with which the barges were laden. One barge went by, two. Andrew looked back toward the basin, thought he saw something moving there, but his vision was cut off by the third barge. Sara was looking that way too, frowning. The third barge went by and there, well out of the basin, was another tug. It had been concealed by the barges and was now travelling fast downstream.

"Sara, do you think . . . ?" began Andrew.

"Yes," she said. "I think that's it."

"What?" said Thatcher, picking up a pair of binoculars. "Where?"

Sara pointed, but before he could bring the binoculars to bear, the last barge had cut off his vision. The tug and another one farther up the road on the near side helped illuminate it. This could well be important, but at the moment, it didn't matter very much because there was no sign of movement in the part he could see: no hansom or four-wheeler went either up it or down it nor were there any belated pedestrians.

Andrew tried to divide his time equally between the grounds and the street outside, watching one for a while, then switching to the other. The night was still as well as dark. Not a leaf stirred either inside or outside Three Oaks and the only sound was Sara's regular, quiet breathing. Time passed. And suddenly he realized he had been looking at one tree for some time—looking at it but not really seeing it—and he also realized that his eyes were starting to close as Sara's had. He shook his head to clear it. He mustn't fall asleep now—he couldn't! He started reciting poetry to himself—all the poems he could remember—to help keep awake. He ran through several ballads and was on *Kubla Khan*, one of his favorites, when his eyes closed again.

He did not know how long he slept or what woke him—possibly the chime on the church clock because, as he opened his eyes, he heard the grandfather clock, which was a minute or two slow, striking on the landing two floors below him. It seemed to have struck only once. Did that mean it was one o'clock? Or was it a quarter after one or two or even three?

He turned to look at Sara. She had not moved, was

lying on her side, eyes closed, breathing softly and regularly. He looked out the window again—at Three Oaks first—and stiffened. There was a change here, possibly a significant one. A light was on now in one of the bedrooms. Of course, he did not know how long it had been on or what it meant. Possibly someone had awakened and, unable to fall asleep again, had lit one of the gas jets. On the other hand . . .

No! It was more than that—it had to be—for there were now two more lights! They were rather faint and while one of them was stationary, the other was moving slowly down through the grounds toward it. Andrew watched them for a moment, then shook Sara gently. Her eyes opened. She looked at him, around the dark attic, then sat up.

"What is it?" she whispered.

He nodded toward the window, and she moved closer to him and looked out.

"Lights," she said. "I don't know where that one is, but the other's coming down from the house."

"I think the first one's somewhere near the greenhouse," said Andrew.

She studied the stationary light. "I think you're right. But who can they be and what are they doing?"

"I don't know who, but they're obviously meeting. There!"

The moving light reached the other, then they both went out.

"Now what?" asked Sara.

"They're together."

"I know. I meant, what do we do?"

"There's nothing we can do except wait, see if we can find out who it is and what they're up to."

Sara sighed. "I wish it weren't so dark—that the moon was out—then we'd be able to see *something*."

Andrew didn't answer. They waited, they could not tell for how long—ten minutes, fifteen?

"I'm afraid . . ." began Andrew.

"Sssh!" said Sara.

Then he heard it too—the clop of a horse's hoofs. They looked toward the street. A dray was moving slowly up it from Wellington Road. The driver was a small man wearing a broken peaked cap, and sitting next to him was a woman wrapped in a shawl, who appeared to be elderly and grey-haired. They only caught a glimpse of them, then the dray had gone by and all they could see was the canvas top that covered its back, the lantern and feed bag that hung from the rear axle.

"Strange," said Andrew, frowning. "I've a feeling I've seen that woman before, but I don't know where."

"That's not all that's strange," said Sara. "What's she doing riding on a dray at this time of night? And what's a dray doing around here anyway?"

"You're right," said Andrew.

They stared after the dray. They could no longer see it, but they could hear the slow plod of the horse's hoofs, the squeak of one ungreased wheel. Then suddenly there was silence.

"It stopped," said Sara. Her eyes widened. "Andrew, do you think it can have anything to do with what's going on inside there?"

"Maybe. It stopped somewhere this side of the gate."

They looked back inside Three Oaks. They could still see nothing, but suddenly, for the first time, they heard something; the sound of footsteps on gravel. The two, whoever they were, had come down to the walk just inside the wall. Then, with no warning, a light flashed, moved over the shrubbery to the wall, then disappeared again. (They realized later that the two night-walkers must have been carrying bull's-eye lanterns, opened, then closed the shutters.) In that momentary gleam of light they could not see the mysterious two, but they could see why they had been moving so slowly and carefully. They were carrying something; a rectangular black wooden box more than six feet long.

"A coffin!" said Andrew. "I think . . . Brother Ibrahim's coffin!"

"You know what's in it, don't you?" said Sara. "A China orange to all of Lombard Street it's the stiff that disappeared!"

"Probably. And now they're going to get rid of it. That's what the dray's waiting for!"

"Do you think Beasley knows?"

"He must!"

diately the tug picked up speed again, began travelling faster than ever.

"Was that a gun?" asked Wyatt.

"Yes," said Andrew, giving him the glasses. "The man with the cape must have threatened the captain, told him he'd shoot him if he stopped."

"Well, we know where we stand now," said Thatcher grimly. "Jack, hang your hat over the gauge. You've got to give us a few more knots."

Again the engineer looked at him, at the gauge. Then, opening the firebox, he threw on shovelful after shovelful of coal. Shuddering like a live thing, the launch responded, and though black smoke was pouring from the tug's smokestack, it was now clear that the launch was the swifter craft. Slowly, yard by yard, she drew closer to the tug.

"Do you have any firearms on board, Inspector?" asked Wyatt.

"No, we haven't. Why?"

The answer came from the tug. Leaning out of the pilot house, the man with the cape raised his hand. There was a flash, a loud report and a bullet drilled a hole in the smokestack just over his head.

"Get down," said Wyatt, pushing Sara and Andrew to the deck. "And stay down!"

"So he's going to cut up rough, is he?" said Thatcher. "All right. Then you've got my word for it that we'll lay him by the heels if we have to follow him to China!"

Spreading his legs wide for better balance, he watched the tug carefully and when the man with the cape raised his hand again, he pushed the tiller over. The launch veered sharply and the second shot missed the launch by several feet, sending up a splash of muddy water.

Now the tugboat captain decided to take a hand in the game. As the launch drew closer and the man with the cape raised his hand for a third shot, he spun the wheel hard over; the tugboat swung to starboard, rammed her nose into a mudbank with such force that the man with the cape went flying and landed sprawling on the forward deck.

"Put me on board her!" said Wyatt.

Reversing his engine, Thatcher brought the launch alongside the tug. Wyatt jumped onto it. As he ran forward, the man with the cape got to his feet and started to raise his gun again, but diving at him, Wyatt brought him crashing down. There was a brief struggle; then, knocking the gun from his hand, Wyatt pinned him to the deck and called, "Got a pair of darbies?"

Thatcher, holding the launch just off the tug's stern, threw him a pair of handcuffs. Wyatt snapped them on and pulled the man to his feet. His hat had been knocked off in the struggle, and now even Sara and Andrew on the launch could see his shaven head and realized he was Brother Ibrahim. At the same time, seeing the old woman by daylight, they recognized her as Mrs. Snyder, mother of the missing girl, Lily.

It was after ten when they arrived back at Wapping. The launch had helped pull the tug off the mudbank, and even though Wyatt did not seem to be having any trouble with the fugitives once he had put the handcuffs on Brother Ibrahim, Thatcher thought he should stand by and so they proceeded up the river together.

As the launch and the tug tied up at the floating dock, the station house door opened and Finch came down the steps.

"Good morning, Inspector," said Thatcher cheerfully. "As you can see, we got them."

"Got who?"

"Why, the people you wanted."

"Who said I wanted them?"

"What?" Thatcher looked at Finch, then at Wyatt, who stood at the tug's stern holding Brother Ibrahim by the arm. "Constable Wyatt."

"He told you I wanted them?"

"Why, yes. Don't you?"

Before Finch could answer, Ibrahim, who had been following this exchange closely, said, "I demand to see Egypt Consul! I demand to know why I handcuffed!"

"I haven't the faintest idea why you've been hand-cuffed," said Finch.

"But the constable here . . ." said Thatcher.

"The constable," said Finch savagely, "is not going to be a constable for very much longer! He was suspended from all duties and confined to quarters several days ago. This is how he followed orders on that. And now we can add this little dido to the other charges against him!" And he gestured toward the fugitives who stood at the stern of the tug.

Thatcher blinked. "I don't understand . . ." he began.

"What's so difficult about it?" said Finch. "I've told you about Wyatt. As for those three there, while I know who two of them are, I haven't a thing against them and as far as I'm concerned you can turn them loose."

11

The Corpse Reappears

Andrew should not have been surprised—he had been aware of Finch's hostility toward Wyatt for some time— but he was. He was so surprised that for a moment he was speechless. Sara, however, had no such disability.

"Why, you sod!" she said. "You meeching, soft-headed slop! You should have your buttons snipped off, you should, and be drummed out of the force!"

"Are you addressing me?" asked Finch.

"You bet your khyber, I am!" As she stepped onto the dock, eyes blazing, and prepared to continue, the station house door opened again and Verna came out followed by a grey-haired man with a close-cropped military mustache. Though Sara had mentioned his name a short while before, it was not until Finch and Thatcher both looked startled and straightened up that Andrew remembered who he was; Divisional Superintendent

Wendell of Scotland Yard, whom he'd met at Bentley's with Lord Lowther after theatre.

"So there you are," said Verna, looking first at Sara and then at Andrew. "Are you all right?"

"Yes and no," said Andrew.

She frowned, but before she could ask him what he meant, Wendell took over.

"Hello there, Finch," he said pleasantly. "Hello, Thatcher. Well, what's all this?" he asked, nodding at Brother Ibrahim and his two companions.

"I don't rightly know, sir," said Thatcher. "According to Constable Wyatt, they're wanted for robbery and murder. But according to Inspector Finch, they're not wanted at all."

"Oh? Would you care to explain, Inspector?"

"I'm afraid I can't, sir," said Finch, "since I don't have a thing against these people. But I think I should tell you that I suspected Wyatt from all duties several days ago and confined him to quarters pending a hearing at which I will bring charges against him for insubordination and for assaulting a superior officer, namely me."

"Hmm. I must say that sounds very serious, Inspector. But in that case, perhaps we should ask Constable Wyatt to explain."

"I'll be glad to, sir," said Wyatt. "But may I make a request?"

"You can certainly make it. Whether I'll grant it is something else again."

"My request is that I be permitted to make my explanation at the scene of the crime—or of one of the crimes. To wit: Three Oaks in St. John's Wood."

"The Marchioness of Medford's place?"

"Yes, sir. I would like the marchioness and her house guest, Mrs. Van Gelder, to be present. They can help me considerably by answering a few questions. And since I will be making accusations against these three individuals here, it seems only right that they should come along too."

"Well, that sounds fair enough. What do you say, Finch?"

"I say it's all nonsense. But if you're prepared to waste your time on it . . ."

"Oh, I am. After all, everyone's entitled to his day in court. Anything else, Constable?"

"That coffin should be brought along, too."

"Right. Will you take care of the details, transportation and all that, Inspector? I think we should proceed there—to Three Oaks—immediately."

It may have been because one of his superiors was involved, but Finch proved quite efficient in this particular exercise. The fact that Fred was there with the landau helped of course—it was he who had taken Verna to Scotland Yard to get the superintendent and then brought both to the police station—and he now drove the family, Wendell and Wyatt back to St. John's Wood. As a result, in a little over an hour, they were all assembled in the salon at Three Oaks and the marchioness was saying, "Yes, of course it's all right. It's just that I'm bewildered. I mean, handcuffs on Brother Ibrahim?"

"It's an outrage!" said Mrs. Van Gelder. "An absolute outrage!"

"Perhaps it is a bit excessive," said the superintendent. "Do you think we might have them off, Finch?"

"I didn't put them on in the first place. Ask Wyatt."

"Since we do have men posted outside, I think we can take a chance on it," said Wyatt, producing a key and opening the handcuffs. "Now may I ask you a few questions, ma'am?"

"If it will clear this up," said the marchioness. "Yes, of course."

"Will you tell us where and how you met Brother Ibrahim?"

"Why, yes. It was last winter in Cairo. Mrs. Van Gelder told me about him, and—"

"You knew Mrs. Van Gelder?"

"No. We met in Cairo. We were staying at the same hotel, were both alone, both widows, and we liked each other. As I said, she told me about him, took me to see him, and I was most impressed. He was such a *spiritual* person." Ibrahim bowed. "And he told me such interesting things."

"What kind of things?"

"About my dead husband. Things no one could possibly know—things he'd said to me—and where he was now, what he was doing in the Great Beyond, and how we were going to be together there."

"And so you invited him to come back to England with you."

"Yes. He was reluctant at first. He said he had his temple and his own work there. But Mrs. Van Gelder joined me in persuading him that we in the west were now ready for the teachings of Ageless Wisdom."

"So you built a temple for him here."

She nodded. "My father had put in the grotto when he landscaped Three Oaks. Brother Ibrahim told me what he wanted done to it—how it should be enlarged and so on—and I did it; and then, after he had sanctified it, we celebrated the mysteries there."

"Who is we?"

"Mrs. Van Gelder and I and friends of mine—ten or twelve of them—who were interested and who Brother Ibrahim thought were ready to participate."

"Will you tell us a little about these mysteries?"

"I don't know," said the marchioness, a little uncertainly.

"No!" said Mrs. Van Gelder sharply. "You can't! Don't forget you took an oath of secrecy."

"That's true," said the marchioness. She looked at Brother Ibrahim, and when he shook his head, she said, "I'm afraid I can't."

"Very well," said Wyatt. "Then I'll tell you. There was incense. There was soft music and chanting and you usually saw something—something strange and inexplicable."

"Yes," whispered the marchioness.

"Did anyone else participate or assist in these mysteries besides you, Mrs. Van Gelder and your friends?"

"Yes. Near the end there *was* someone else—a young woman whom Brother Ibrahim had trained as a temple dancer."

"What do you mean by 'near the end'?"

"She . . . she only came two or three times. Then . . . well, we stopped performing the mysteries."

"Why? What happened to her?"

The marchioness started. "How did you know that something happened to her?"

"Never mind. Will you tell us what happened?"

"This is outrageous!" said Mrs. Van Gelder. "Is this your famous British justice? I can assure you that nothing like it could happen in America!"

"Like what, Mrs. Van Gelder?" asked Wyatt.

"Questioning someone like this with no lawyer present and without charging them with anything!"

"I doubt that there's any intention of charging the marchioness with anything," said Wendell mildly. "Is that correct, Constable?" And when Wyatt nodded, "At the moment, she is merely assisting in an investigation."

"And what about Brother Ibrahim and these other two people, this man and poor old woman? Why are they being held?"

"There certainly seems to be good reason for asking Brother Ibrahim some questions," said the superintendent. "He was trying to flee the country, and I am informed that he not only menaced a tugboat captain, he fired at the Thames Police when they tried to stop him."

"Because did not understand!" said Ibrahim. "Because did not know were police—thought were river pirates!"

"Didn't the tugboat captain tell you it was the police?" asked Wyatt. "The launch carried a green light."

"Don't know. I told you, did not understand—too upset. As for going away, leaving country, it was because . . ."

"We'll come to that," said Wendell. "In the meantime, I think the constable should be permitted to continue."

"Thank you, sir," said Wyatt. "I suspect that this will be rather difficult, ma'am," he said, turning to the marchioness again. "But will you now tell us what happened to the young girl who participated in your mysteries?"

"I . . ." began the marchioness, looking unhappily first at Mrs. Van Gelder and then at Brother Ibrahim.

"No, Maria," said Mrs. Van Gelder firmly. "Remember we discussed it all thoroughly."

Wyatt did not wait for the marchioness's refusal. "Let me ask you another question, then. Was the young woman's name Lily Snyder?"

"Why, yes. It was. How did you know that?"

"It was fairly obvious. She was the young woman who

disappeared somewhere in St. John's Wood a little over a week ago, and I spent some time searching for her. Now will you tell us what happened to her?" Then, as the marchioness still hesitated, "Would it make any difference to you if I told you that this lady here," and he pointed to the old woman who sat next to Ibrahim, "was her mother?"

"Oh," said the marchioness. "I wondered. It seemed to me that I'd seen her with Inspector Finch and . . . Yes, it does make a difference, and I will tell you. She was killed!"

"Lily Snyder?"

"Yes."

Unconsciously, Andrew's eyes had gone to the old woman, and though it was difficult to see her face, it was his impression that her expression had not changed. Why? Was this something she already knew?

"Will you tell us how she was killed?"

"It was during one of the mysteries—an evocation. We had gone through the early ritual, and the girl was dancing. We were hoping for some kind of manifestation—Isis or Hathor, one of the goddesses. Instead . . ." She shuddered. "I still get nightmares about it—Seth appeared!"

"Seth?"

"Yes. The evil, animal god. He was huge, apelike, with fangs and claws. He seized her, she screamed, and the torches went out."

"Why do you say she was killed?"

"Because, when the torches were lit again, she was gone—they were both gone—and we were all spattered with blood."

"You never saw her again?"

"No. No one did."

"I see." Wyatt's voice was curiously gentle. "What did you do about it?"

"Nothing."

"Nothing?"

"No. Brother Ibrahim explained that it was no one's fault—that sometimes the forces of evil were too powerful to control. But he said it would be a mistake to go to the police. That they would not understand. So we did nothing."

"Not even when the stories about the missing girl appeared in the newspapers and this woman here, her mother, began haunting St. John's Wood, searching for her?"

"No. Not until we got those notes."

"What notes?"

"We all got them—everyone who had been at the grotto that night. But I think mine was the first."

"Do you have the note?"

"No, I destroyed it afterward, but I remember most of it. I said, 'There is blood on your hands—the blood of an innocent girl.' Then . . . I forget exactly how it was phrased, but the idea was that if I wished to make amends I was to put a thousand pounds into a bag and throw it over the garden wall in a certain place and at a certain time of night. If I did that, whoever had written the note would remain silent about it."

"Did you do it?"

"Yes, I did."

Andrew suddenly remembered the strange whistle he had heard the night he had come home from school. Could that have been when it happened? Wyatt's next question seemed to confirm this.

"Was this before Miss Tillett's jewels were stolen?" he asked.

"Yes."

"Was that related in any way to what you've been telling us?"

"No. Unless . . . well, in a way, it might have been. Because right after that Augusta—Mrs. Van Gelder—got a note that said if she didn't have the money, she could give them her jewels. And she said she wouldn't mind doing that because afterwards she could claim that they'd been stolen as Miss Tillett's had been. That way she could collect the insurance and not lose anything by it."

"Just a second," said Mrs. Van Gelder angrily. "Are you accusing me of trying to cheat the insurance company?"

"Well, you must admit that you did mislead them, Augusta—and also the police—when you said your jewels had been stolen. Because they weren't. You threw them over the wall in a bag, just as I did the money, according to the directions in a note."

"And did anyone else do that same thing," asked Wyatt, "give the blackmailer jewels and claim they had been stolen?"

"Yes," said the marchioness. "At least, I think so. Because Mrs. Van Gelder suggested the idea to everyone who had been here the night the girl was killed."

"I think that, sir," said Wyatt to the superintendent, "accounts for the wave of jewel robberies. All except Miss Tillett's. I believe that if those involved are questioned, they will admit that their jewels were not stolen, but that they were given to the blackmailer to purchase his silence."

"You say all except Miss Tillett's?"

"Yes. Her jewels—or rather the Denham diamonds, which were in her possession—were actually stolen."

"I suppose," said Finch, speaking for the first time, "you not only know how they were stolen, but who stole them and who the blackmailer is."

"Yes, I think so," said Wyatt.

"Before we get to that," said Mrs. Van Gelder, "there are several points I should like to have cleared up. I shall of course see a lawyer about the way I have been defamed and slandered here. But there is something else I insist on knowing right now. Did you say that there was a murder involved in all this?"

"I did," said Wyatt.

"I assume you mean the murder of this Lily Snyder who disappeared."

"Why, no," said Wyatt. "She was not murdered nor did she disappear. She's right here." He had been standing in front of the elderly Mrs. Snyder, who sat huddled in her chair. Now, turning suddenly, he pulled off first her shawl and then a grey wig that covered her dark hair. As she gasped and shrank back, he used the shawl to wipe away enough of the grease paint to show the young face underneath.

"You're right!" said the marchioness. "That is the girl! But now I'm more confused than ever. What actually happened that night? Why did she pretend to disappear, and . . ."

"I'll explain that later," said Wyatt. "What I'd like to do now is go into the matter of the murder."

"Murder of who?" asked Finch.

"The best way to answer that is to show you the body. If you would accompany me into the garden . . ."

"A question," said Finch. "Is this the famous corpse that your two young friends claimed they saw and that disappeared?"

"Yes."

"And you know where it is?"

"I think so."

"This should be very interesting," said Finch with rather ponderous sarcasm. He called in a constable, instructed him to keep watch on Ibrahim, Lily Snyder and the small, as yet unidentified man, and followed the others—including the marchioness and Mrs. Van Gelder —out the french door and down through the garden.

Parr, the gnomelike head gardener, was working near the greenhouse with one of his assistants. At Wyatt's request, the marchioness summoned them and they came along.

"Just a blooming minute," said Finch when Wyatt paused in front of the same bush they had dug up before. "Are you suggesting . . . ?"

"Yes," said Wyatt. Then to Parr, "Would you dig here, please?"

"Again?" said Parr.

"Yes, please."

Parr looked at him, at Finch, who was grinning smugly, then, jerking his head at his assistant, the two of them got spades and set to work. For the second time they lifted out the bush, Parr's precious *Indicum-Roseum*, then began digging in earnest. Since the earth had been recently turned and there were two of them digging, it took almost no time for them to go down three feet or so. At this point they stepped into the hole and continued digging, the undergardener steadily and stolidly and Parr with the expression of a man who is humoring a backward child. He stepped on his spade, driving it deep into the soft earth, then his expression changed.

"There be something here," he said.

"I thought there might be," said Wyatt. "I suggest that

you work carefully now. And I also suggest that you ladies and Sara and Andrew move back because I'm afraid that what we're going to bring up is not going to be a very pleasant sight."

Sara and Andrew did not move, and though Verna, the marchioness and Mrs. Van Gelder did draw back, they kept their eyes on the two men in the excavation. They had put their spades aside and were working with their bare hands. Finally, bracing themselves, they heaved together and lifted something large and heavy to the edge of the hole. Wyatt, Finch and Wendell reached down and helped them, and when they stepped back, there at the edge of the excavation was the body of the man with the brutal face that Sara and Andrew had seen several nights before outside the wall of Three Oaks.

"But that," said the marchioness wondering, "that looks like . . ."

"You will all stay where you are," said Mrs. Van Gelder in a flat, hard voice. "No one will move."

They all looked at her incredulously—all except Wyatt. She had stepped back several paces, and she had a short-barreled pistol of very large calibre in her hand.

"You," she said to Sara, her eyes as cold and steady as the gun barrel, "come here."

Sara hesitated, then walked toward her. Mrs. Van Gelder took her by the hand.

"Good," she said, pressing the gun to the back of Sara's head. "Now you will all do exactly as I say."

"That won't get you anywhere, Mrs. Van Gelder," said Wyatt quietly. "Or should I say Mrs. Stokey?"

"Oh, yes, it will. It will get Doc and me out of the country. Or this quite nice child will have her head blown off. Now we will all go back up to the house, where I will tell you what I want done and how. And I am sure that I need not warn you that if one of you makes a move I don't like—Aah!"

She broke off, her voice rising as a large hand reached around from behind her, seized her wrist and bore down on it.

"What bad manners some of you Americans have," said Beasley. "Hasn't anyone ever told you that pointing guns at people is not only dangerous, but downright rude? No, you don't!" he said as she turned, tried to bring the gun to bear on him. He twisted her wrist sharply, and she cried out and dropped the gun. Verna, meanwhile, had grabbed Sara and pulled her away.

"Well done," said Wyatt. "May I present my friend Baron Beasley, who has been extremely helpful even before this?" Then as Beasley bowed, "I think Inspector Finch would like that gun if you will keep hold of Mrs. Stokey. And now perhaps we should follow her suggestion and return to the house while we tie up the remaining loose ends."

12

The Loose Ends

"There's nothing very strange about it," said Beasley. He glared at the small man who sat between Lily Snyder and Ibrahim. "The mickey he slipped me had me out like the tide till about ten this ack emma. When I came to, I went over to the Tillett house. My young friends weren't there and neither was Miss Tillett, but Sara's mother gave me some breakfast and something for my head. Then, a little while ago, the coachman came in and said he'd just taken Miss Tillett, the young 'uns and Wyatt next door and that the police were bringing the flash-coves they'd been chasing. So I thought I'd amble-ramble over. When I got there, you were all watching that stiff being dug up, didn't notice me."

"Particularly Mrs. Stokey," said Wyatt. "Which was a lucky thing. I assume that by now everyone knows what happened, how and why."

"Certainly not," said the marchioness. "If I was confused before, I'm completely baffled now."

"Perhaps you'd better run through it from square one," said Wendell. "I gather it began as a very elaborate confidence game."

"Exactly, sir. What the Americans call a scam. Our friend here," he indicated Ibrahim, "is an American. I'm not sure what his real name is, but he's known to the police as Doc Stokey."

"When you say known, I take it he's not a doctor of medicine."

"No, sir. He's apparently quite a good magician and illusionist, had a travelling magic and medicine show. That is, he sold various kinds of nostrums and cure-alls. This led him and his wife into the confidence game. They did quite well at it until one man whom they'd fleeced went to the New York Police. He was found dead the next day, and when the police tried to question Stokey, they discovered that he and his wife had disappeared."

"They'd come here?"

"I think so. Beasley believes they were here for about six months to get the lay of the land, work out their scam and make their connections. Then they took off for Egypt where Stokey became Brother Ibrahim and Mrs. Stokey became Mrs. Van Gelder."

"This brings us to what the marchioness has told us. Can you tell us what actually happened on the night she described?"

"I believe so. Lily had been cast in the role of one of the temple handmaidens or dancing girls. She had danced once or twice as part of the so-called evocation. On that particular night they also made use of a former prize-fighter, rampsman and demander named 'Mauler' Cobb."

"He played the god, Seth?"

"Yes. It would have been a simple matter for a skilled illusionist to arrange for his appearance and his disappearance with Lily. Stokey was now ready to demand blackmail from all those who had been there that evening. In order to exert additional pressure on them, he had Lily playing her own bereaved mother, asking the newspapers for help and castigating the police."

"That's clear," said Wendell. "And I can understand why the marchioness might have paid up. She would not only have felt guilty, responsible because the incident took place here, but would have been advised to pay up by her friend and house guest, Mrs. Van Gelder. But what about the others?"

"Some probably felt as guilty as the marchioness. Some were probably willing to pay up, not because they felt guilty but because they didn't want anyone to know that they'd been involved in anything as bizarre as that. But one of the big factors—and this is where Stokey showed himself to be really creative—was the fact that, except for the marchioness, it would not cost them anything. They could turn over their jewels, claim they had been stolen, and be reimbursed by the insurance companies."

"Yes, I can see that. However you said that Miss Tillett's jewels—or rather the Denham diamonds that were in her possession—were actually stolen. Is that correct?"

"It is. This established the pattern that would allow the others to *pretend* that their jewels had been stolen, and it also created a false scent, for it had all of us looking for a gang of jewel thieves."

"This is all very interesting," said Finch. "But if you'll excuse my saying so, a lot of it's talk. Can you tell us just *how* the Denham diamonds were stolen if it was an outside job?"

"Yes, I think so," said Wyatt. He turned to Sara and Andrew. "Do either of you recognize this man?" he asked, indicating the small man who sat between Ibrahim and Lily.

They shook their heads.

"We both felt that there was something familiar about him, but . . . no," said Andrew.

Wyatt had apparently rubbed some lead from his pencil on his forefinger. Now, with two swift strokes, he drew a large mustache on the small man's face.

"Now do you recognize him?"

"The organ grinder!" said Sara. "Wait a minute. You don't mean he sent the monkey up to steal the diamonds?"

Wyatt smiled. "I think he would have liked to, but . . . no. That would take too much training. However, it wouldn't be difficult to get a monkey to climb up the front of a house carrying a cord that could be used to pull up a rope, which he could then climb. Because, unless I'm very much mistaken, this gentleman is Jocko Nimm, a well-known cat burglar or second-story man."

"But how did he know about the Denham diamonds?" asked Verna. "Know that they were there?"

"He didn't," said Wyatt. "That was a piece of unexpected luck. They needed a robbery that would attract attention, picked you because you're well-known and would certainly be written about. Actresses usually have jewels, and of course you'd wear them at an opening night party."

"That's true," said Verna. "I don't have much jewelry, but I would have worn what I had if I hadn't worn the Denham diamonds."

"I assume it was Nimm who went around collecting the jewels from the other victims," said Wendell. "But what about the murder? Am I correct in also assuming that the body we dug up was that of the prizefighter, Mauler Cobb?"

"Yes, sir," said Wyatt. "My guess is that while Cobb

had only been engaged to play the god Seth on the night Lily was to disappear, he suspected that what he had done was part of something very big, especially when the stories about the jewel robberies began appearing in the press. I therefore believe that he, in turn, tried to blackmail Stokey, saying that he would talk unless he got a share of the loot. So Stokey served him as he did the man in New York—pretended to agree, got him to come here to Three Oaks late at night, then, while Cobb waited to be paid off, slipped a knife between his ribs."

"You're going to have a hard—a very hard time—proving any of this!" said Stokey, exchanging his Egyptian accent for a more natural American one.

"Perhaps. Perhaps not," said Wyatt.

"You're all taking this very matter-of-factly," said Verna. "Speaking for myself, I think the way you've unravelled this very complicated plot, Constable, is absolutely brilliant." Then, as Wyatt bowed modestly, "May I ask when you first suspected the truth?"

"Well, I did think there was something a little odd about the organ grinder. His manner and accent were very good, but his clothes seemed a little too new. When your house was robbed, I was convinced it was an outside job—the clues all pointed to someone coming in through the window. And while I didn't see how anyone could have climbed up, I remembered the monkey, realized *he* could have done so—and also realized that pretending to be an organ grinder was the perfect disguise for someone who wanted to study a place before robbing it."

" 'Strewth, it is that!" said Beasley. "When you stand in front of it, lamping it, folks'll think you're looking out for them as might toss you some rhino."

"Exactly," said Wyatt. "The next step in my suspicions came when I met friend Stokey as Brother Ibrahim and he showed us his tattoo."

"What was wrong with it?" asked Stokey.

"The falcon and the Eye of Horus didn't quite match —as if they had been done at different times by different tattoo artists. I finally decided that the falcon had originally been an American eagle that had been done some time ago, and since tattooing can never be completely removed, you had someone work it over, do the Eye of Horus above it and hoped you could pass the whole thing off as Egyptian. But the clincher was two items that were found, one behind a tree near where Cobb was murdered and the other near where his body was found here in Three Oaks."

"What were they?" asked Wendell.

"I don't suppose you have them with you?" Wyatt asked Andrew.

"If you mean those cigarette butts, no," said Andrew. "They're in my room."

"Is there something special about them?" asked Wendell.

"Yes," said Wyatt. "In the first place they indicated that whoever hid behind the tree and killed Cobb had access to Three Oaks and probably buried him. But there was something else about them that was very significant. Will you describe them, Andrew?"

"Well, the tobacco was kind of loose and there was something odd about the paper . . ." He suddenly remembered the cowboy he had watched making a cigarette at the Wild West Show. "I know! They're the butts of the kind of cigarettes that cowboys smoke when they roll their own! That means that whoever made and smoked them must have been an American, and . . ."

Mrs. Stokey suddenly struck her husband a stinging slap in the face.

"You!" she said. "I'll be damned if I'm going to hang because you're a fool!"

Stokey reeled back, then leaped at her, took her by the throat and began choking her.

"Now none of that," said Wendell as Wyatt and Finch pulled the raging Stokey away from her. "Perhaps you'd better take them away, Inspector. Do you have enough men to handle them?"

"Yes, sir," said Finch. "We came here in a Black Maria and I had it wait. But before I go I'd like to ask Wyatt how he knew where that body was."

"Stokey told me."

"I take it that's one of your varsity jokes."

"In a way. I suspected he had something in mind when

he told us it was buried under that bush. He must have had it hidden somewhere nearby, probably in the compost pit. But after we had dug down and found nothing, that became the best place in all London to hide it. Because, having looked there once, who would think of looking there again?"

"All right," said Stokey with sudden decision. "I'll grant you've been pretty smart about a lot of things. But there's one thing you don't know and that's where the jewels are. Now I'll make a deal with you. If you'll go easy on me, and"—nodding at Wendell—"I'll take his word for it that you will, I'll tell you where they are."

"Poor Stokey," said Wyatt. "I really feel quite bad about this, but of course we all know where the jewels are."

"What do you mean, we know?" said Finch. "Who's 'we'?"

"Why, all of us," said Wyatt. "For instance, don't you know, Sara?"

Sara hesitated a moment, and Andrew sensed that she didn't know, anymore than he did. But he also knew that if Wyatt felt that they should be able to guess, then they should. Then, suddenly it came to him. At the same time, Sara said, "Yes, I think I do. I couldn't imagine why they took that coffin with them. At first I thought they had that body in it. But when we found they didn't . . . Well, the only reason for taking it must have been because the jewels are hidden in it."

"Damn you!" said Stokey, his face dark with rage. "All of you! I—"

His face just as flushed, Finch quick-marched him out of the room, and two constables followed, leading out the others.

"*Is* that where the jewels are?" asked Verna.

"From his reaction, I would suspect so," said Wyatt. "If the marchioness will have someone bring us some tools, we'll open it and see."

"While we're waiting," said Verna, "will you tell us how you collected all that information, especially about two Americans, when you were confined to your quarters during these last few days?"

"Beasley got it for me. I spent over a year in the United States after I left Cambridge. While I was in New York I made a point of getting a letter of introduction to the police commissioner. I had Beasley send him a cable in my name asking about a confidence man with a tattooed chest. Back came a cable with a description of Stokey and his wife, saying they were wanted."

"Was that what was on the paper you threw out the section-house window?" asked Andrew.

"Yes. That and some questions about a cat burglar and a missing prizefighter."

"Once I had their descriptions, finding out who they were was easy," said Beasley. "It was what I had to do besides, play night watchman, that gave me the pip."

A footman came in with a box of tools and Wyatt and

Beasley set to work on the coffin.

"You don't suppose there's something really horrid in there, do you?" asked the marchioness in an unsteady voice.

"No, ma'am. But of course that was part of Stokey's strategy, the reason for the coffin. The tugboat captain had been told that it contained the body of Stokey's brother who had died of cholera and wished to be buried at sea. Fear of contagion, added to respect for the dead, made it unlikely that anyone would wish to look into it. However . . ."

The coffin lid creaked open. Wyatt lifted out some bulky objects wrapped in a blanket. When he unwrapped them, the marchioness gasped.

"But that . . . that's my silver! The Medford punch bowl, cups, candlesticks—"

"They needed something to give weight to the coffin," said Wyatt, "make it seem there was a body in it. So why not improve the shining hour with something valuable?"

He reached into the coffin again, pulled up the cloth lining and brought out a chamois bag. The first thing they saw when he opened it were the Denham diamonds.

"Well done!" said Wendell. "Though I must say that having Miss Sara here guess where they were when Finch clearly didn't have a clue himself must have been a little hard for him to take."

"I suspect it was," said Wyatt. "But, if you don't mind, I won't apologize for it. Because I've had to take

a good deal from him. In fact, if it weren't for Miss Tillett, Beasley and my two young friends here, I'd be off
the force now. Though as far as that goes, I suppose . . ."

"Now, now, you know better than that," said Wendell. "I wouldn't dream of letting you go—though we'll
have to think of some tactful way of arranging for your
transfer to the C.I.D. But you're right about your two
young friends. What do you propose to do about them?"

"I don't know, sir. Take them out to dinner to celebrate, I suppose—along with Miss Tillett and Beasley
here. Because I've got to make sure I can call on them
for help if I need it in any future cases."

He smiled at them, and conscious of the emotion behind the smile, they smiled back.